The window shattered as a bullet hit it. Two inches from Maggie's head.

Maggie screamed and pulled a shrieking Rory from the car.

"Run!" Dan bellowed. With a runner's sprint, she hurtled toward the trees. Dan was on her heels, cradling baby Siobhan tightly in his arms.

A car screeched into the parking lot, bullets spewing from the open window. Dan looked back in time to see a bullet hit a gas pump.

"Faster!" he barked. Ducking his head, he forced himself to hold the baby tighter and push forward.

The pump exploded. Dan yelled as the back of his leather jacket ignited. "Take her!"

Maggie grabbed the baby and Dan dived for the ground, rolling until the flames were out. He thanked God with all his heart that his jacket had taken the worst of the fire. He had, however, twisted his knee when he dived to the ground. Forcing himself to stand, he limped next to Maggie.

He had never seen anything more beautiful than her tired face, scratch_____ uninjured. And the _____ down their faces. B_____ them down. Not like_____

Dana R. Lynn grew up in Illinois. She met her husband at a wedding and told her parents she had met her future husband. Nineteen months later, they were married. Today, they live in rural Pennsylvania with their three children and enough pets to open a petting zoo. In addition to writing, she works as an educational interpreter for the deaf and is active in several ministries at her church.

Books by Dana R. Lynn

Love Inspired Suspense

Presumed Guilty
Interrupted Lullaby

Visit the Author Profile page at Harlequin.com.

INTERRUPTED LULLABY

DANA R. LYNN

⟨H⟩ HARLEQUIN® LOVE INSPIRED® SUSPENSE

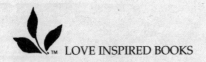

LOVE INSPIRED BOOKS

Recycling programs
for this product may
not exist in your area.

ISBN-13: 978-0-373-44724-4

Interrupted Lullaby

www.Harlequin.com

Printed in U.S.A.

Teach me, Lord, your way that I may walk in your truth, single-hearted and revering your name.
—Psalms 86:11

To my mom,
who taught me about unconditional love and sacrifice.

And to my Lord and Savior.
May this work bring glory to Your name.

Acknowledgments

I am so grateful for the many people who supported me so
that this labor of love could happen. First, to my husband,
Brad, and our kids. Thanks for allowing me time in my
writing cave/dining room table. It meant so much!
Amy and Dee, my dearest friends...you kept me sane.
My critique partners and fellow Killer Voices authors,
how would I have done this without bouncing ideas off you?

A special thanks to my editor Elizabeth Mazer
and my agent Mary Sue Seymour. I have been blessed
by your guidance and humbled by your faith in me.

ONE

"I know where Margaret Slade is."

Lieutenant Dan Willis held the phone receiver away from his ear and stared at it, shocked. His colleagues Lieutenant Jace Tucker and Chief Paul Kennedy halted their lively discussion on the upcoming football game to watch him. Jace raised his eyebrows. Paul leaned forward. Dan pressed a button, putting the caller on speaker.

"Margaret Slade, you said? You've seen her?" Dan nodded as Jace whistled silently. Maggie Slade had vanished more than eighteen months ago in suspicious circumstances. Although he had never stopped looking for her, he had all but given up hope of ever finding her. Alive, anyway.

"Yes, Officer." The caller's voice quavered. In Dan's mind, he was picturing someone's sweet white-haired granny. "I went to the post office two days ago. Maybe three. I saw some of them missing persons flyers. I thought one of them looked real familiar. It wasn't until this mornin' when my neighbor was puttin' out her trash that I realized it was her."

"Are you sure? How long has she lived there?" *Calm*

down, Dan reminded himself. *This could be another dead end.* Dan couldn't help it, though. Hope rose up in his soul.

"She's not the real owner. Name's Mary Connors. Hair's different than the photo, and she keeps to herself. She moved in almost a year ago, renting, I suppose. I would go ask her, but her car's not in the driveway."

"If she does return, please don't confront her with your suspicions. And don't let on that you've talked to the police."

The caller agreed, her tone colored with reluctance. People loved to get involved in police business. Especially if they felt they could accept some of the credit. Maybe he was cynical, but he'd seen it happen before.

Dan quickly took down the address and hung up, his adrenaline flowing. Jace leaned over his shoulder to peer at the address. When Jace reached down to pick up the paper, the plain gold wedding band on his left hand flashed as the morning sunlight streaming through the window caught it.

"Huh. Never heard of the place," he mused.

"I have," Dan told him. "It's right outside of Pittsburgh. Big enough to get lost in, but small enough to not feel like a city. Chief?"

Paul nodded. "Yeah, it's pretty quiet here today. You go ahead and check this out. But do it quietly. If she gets any clue we might be onto her, she might take off again."

Unasked was the question of why was she still in hiding. Maggie had been a juror in a high-profile murder trial almost six years earlier. Some of the jurors had been murdered a year and a half ago. Maggie had disappeared. Did she know she was safe now? That the murderers had been caught? Or was she hiding for another reason altogether?

"Would you call Chief Garraway?" Dan threw over his shoulder as he headed out of the room. The LaMar Pond department he belonged to now had been collaborating with his old precinct in Pittsburgh on the case. Although Maggie was from LaMar Pond, their past three leads had taken them to Pittsburgh. The two precincts had decided that it was in the best interests of all involved if they worked together. Dan had taken the position as the liaison. He caught Paul's nod. Good. He was outta here.

Two and a half hours later, he coasted down the quiet suburban street. His right foot hovered over the brake pedal, ready to tap it at a moment's notice. Leaning forward in his seat, he narrowed his eyes as he scanned the house numbers: 52414…52416… There! 52418 Cherry Lane. That was it. The driveway was still empty. Turning the wheel, he parked his unmarked car on the opposite side of the road. To keep him from looking suspicious, he pulled a map out of the side pocket of the door as a prop and spread it out over the steering wheel. Then he waited.

A yawn caught him by surprise. It figured. He should have known his insomnia would catch up with him. He took a sip of coffee from his travel mug. Hopefully the caffeine would help him remain alert. In an effort to keep himself busy, he reviewed the facts of the case.

The anonymous caller had claimed she recognized Maggie Slade from the missing persons flyers in the post office. There was always the chance she was mistaken. It had happened before. The picture used in the flyers had been from her passport. It was at least three years old. Lots of changes could have happened in that time. He planned to be cautious.

The one fact that kept going around in his mind was that the caller had reported that the woman in question was known as Mary Connors. Not very original. Anyone who was really interested could find out that Maggie's full name was Margaret Mary Slade. And that her mother had been Anna O'Connor before she married. Nope, it didn't take a detective to figure out how she had come by the alias. Now all he had to do was sit back and wait for her to appear.

Dan sat still, his eyes vigilant. He scanned the street and then turned his narrowed gaze back on the house, checking for any sort of movement. A car turned onto the street. He kept his posture casual, even though he wanted to sit forward. No use giving himself away.

The car was at least eight years old, a dark blue four-door sedan. Nothing fancy. In fact, no one would look twice at it. It passed him. He put his cell phone to his ear and moved a finger along the map. Anyone looking at him would think he was trying to get directions.

A car backfired. Dan jumped, bumping his head on the roof.

"Idiot. It's just a car. Not a gun," he muttered, disgusted with himself. He hadn't always jumped at loud noises. Just since his second tour in Afghanistan. For a brief moment, his heart sped up as he recalled a burning house. A woman's voice shrieking through the flames. His gut churned. No. He refused to be drawn into thinking about the past. He had a job to do. He forced himself to focus his attention on the vehicle approaching.

The car slowed, stopped briefly and then continued to swerve into the driveway.

Dan ran the license plate number through the database. The vehicle was registered to a Miss Wendy Stroup. The owner of the house. A registered nurse. Her background check showed nothing shady. He scanned the picture of Miss Stroup. Small and blonde, aged twenty-eight. The car door opened. A young woman exited the vehicle. Definitely not Wendy Stroup. It was hard to tell her age, but she could have been twenty-seven. Was that Maggie? Her hair was shoulder length, medium brown. Not the black curls from her photo. Still, hair was easy to change. Her face was thinner than it was in her picture. But was it her?

A jogger made his way down the street. He passed the young woman and tossed her a single wave. She gave him a slight wave and a somewhat forced smile back.

And that was when he knew.

Her smile was the one he'd seen in the pictures of the woman he'd been trying to find for the past eighteen months.

As soon as the jogger passed, the woman hurried to the trunk of her car and lugged out a stroller. A stroller? None of his information suggested a child. She flicked her wrists. The stroller sprang open, and she locked it in place. Whoa. A double stroller. His mouth dropped open as he watched her open the back door of the vehicle. She retrieved one sleeping baby, probably close to a year old, and deposited him in the stroller. Then she repeated the action, this time lifting out a little girl. Before she could place the child in the stroller, the baby girl let out a holler. There was nothing he could do to prevent the grin tugging at his lips. That kid had powerful lungs. Even with the windows up, he could hear her. Maggie's tense face softened. She pulled a pacifier out of a diaper bag and plopped it into the child's mouth. Peace resumed. She snuggled the baby close for a few seconds, then dropped a light kiss on her head and placed her in the stroller.

Her movements grew jerky. Agitated. The woman was nervous. If she was in hiding, she might feel exposed out in the open like this. He would. She pushed the stroller at a jog up the driveway and around the back of the house. A minute later, the blinds in the front window twitched.

He sent off a brief text to Paul, letting him know what was happening.

Chief Garraway would be interested in the developments of this case, seeing as he was in her jurisdiction. Knowing how much she detested texting, he dialed her personal cell number. He knew if he dialed the office number, it would probably go to her voice mail.

She answered on the second ring.

"Garraway."

"Willis here, Chief," he identified himself. "I found her."

He could hear Chief Garraway suck in a breath. "Is she alive?"

"Yes, ma'am. But it seems we were missing some information."

"What information, Willis? Don't play games. Just spit it out."

Dan grimaced. Better just say it and weather the explosion.

"She has a couple of babies with her. Twins."

Silence. That didn't bode well. Then Chief Garraway's voice exploded across the line.

"Twins! We checked all the hospitals, didn't we? How could a juror from a high-profile case go missing for over a year, then waltz into a hospital, *give birth to twins*, then walk out again without us being any the wiser? Can you explain that to me, Lieutenant?"

Dan sighed. "No, Chief. I can't explain it."

"Are they hers?"

"I can't say for sure, ma'am, but my gut says yeah, they're hers. I haven't made contact yet."

"All right. Keep me posted." She ended the call.

Dan leaned over slightly and slid his phone into the back pocket of his jeans. His hair fell over his eyes. He shook his head, knocking the hair back. He'd never intended to let it grow this long. It was starting to annoy him, so he'd probably cut it when this case was over. He'd probably shave his short beard, too. Right now he had a job to do. Time to meet Miss Maggie and find out why she had disappeared all those months ago.

He reached back and grabbed a leather jacket from the rear seat and put it on. Zipped, it hid the holster with his service revolver. He set off at a casual stroll. Remembering Maggie's secretive posture, he walked around to the back door. He might have a better shot at getting her to open her door if she didn't feel as though any passersby could see them talking.

The back door was opened a crack. That was surprising. A woman that wary, he would have assumed she'd have the door shut and bolted.

A scream inside the house jolted him from his thoughts. A woman's scream. Followed by the distinct sound of a slap. The woman cried out in pain.

"Where is it hidden?" This was a man's voice, speaking in a menacing snarl.

Dan broke into a run and burst into the house. Two people were locked in a furious struggle.

With a cry, the woman shoved her elbow into the man's abdomen. He grunted and his hold loosened. She broke away. Her assailant grabbed a fistful of her brown hair and yanked.

Her hair fell off. She had been wearing a wig.

"Police!" Dan yelled, holding his service revolver in front of him. The assailant jerked around and immediately switched targets. Thrusting Maggie aside, he lunged at Dan with a bellow, a large hunting knife in one hand. Dan aimed but was unable to shoot without risking hitting Maggie. In seconds, the assailant was upon him, the wicked knife catching the light as it slashed down.

A burning sensation in his side alerted Dan that he had been stabbed. No time to worry about that now. His attacker was strong but clearly had no training. Dan, on the other hand, had specialized military training—training he hadn't needed to use in several years. But now it kicked in as automatically as if a switch had been flipped. In short order, he had the attacker handcuffed and seated on the ground while he called in to the station to report the situation.

He was aware of Maggie running to check on the children still strapped in the stroller. Listening to the dispatcher, he twisted around to watch her. Maggie had taken a protective stance in front of the stroller, her glare hot and fierce. A grin threatened to form at her resemblance to a protective mama bear. He squelched it. Pretty sure she wouldn't appreciate it in the current situation.

"I'm sending a black-and-white to your location,

Lieutenant Willis," the slightly nasal voice of the dispatcher informed him.

"Glad to hear it. Tell them to come around to the back door." Dan snapped his phone shut and slipped it into his back pocket. That done, he turned to face the woman he had been searching for—Maggie Slade, aka Mary Connors. Her black curls were starting to slip from the bobby pins. Her skin was pale, but her dark blue eyes were alert. Close up he couldn't believe he had doubted it was her.

"Maggie, I'm Lieutenant Dan Willis with the LaMar Pond Police Department. I've been searching for you for a long time."

It hardly seemed possible, but her face paled further.

Maggie retreated several steps before realizing there was no place to run. No way to grab her babies and escape. She was trapped.

And confused.

The jogger, a man who had been waving at her for weeks, was sitting on the floor, handcuffed, cursing and spewing ugly threats at her. He had followed her into the house, sneaked in while she had been setting the brake on the stroller and then attacked. If it hadn't been for the policeman standing in front of her, she was certain she would have been killed. Her eyes went to the knife lying on the floor. She shuddered.

She had been saved by a cop. A cop from LaMar Pond. It could be a trick. Cops were clever. She didn't know which ones she could trust. Was this cop one of the good guys? Or was he connected to the man who had killed Phillip?

The cop glared at the man sitting on the floor. "You

can stop that right now. I'm gonna read you your rights, and then you're going for a ride to jail. So you can sit and think about the error of your ways."

Maggie was shocked when her would-be killer obeyed, although his eyes continued to shoot pure venom at Maggie and her rescuer.

What was the cop's name again? Williams?

"Detective Williams," she began but stopped when he shook his head.

"Willis, ma'am. Lieutenant Willis." He moved his right arm but suddenly sucked in a breath and winced. He lifted his elbow away from his body, angling his head so he could look at his side. His leather jacket gaped open. That's when she noticed the blood seeping from a wound on his right side.

"You're hurt! Did he stab you?" Her eyes flicked from the offending knife back to his side. The stain was spreading across his T-shirt. An ugly chuckle sounded from the attacker. Both Maggie and Lieutenant Willis ignored the man. It was difficult to see the extent of the injury because of the leather jacket he wore. "I didn't hear you call for an ambulance."

A fleeting expression crossed his face—annoyance, embarrassment?—before it once again smoothed out.

"I'll take care of it, ma'am. No need for you to worry about it."

The words were no sooner out of his mouth than he swayed. Maggie leaped forward, grabbed his left arm and hauled him over to a chair. Relying on her first-aid training, she grabbed a towel from the basket of clean laundry on the kitchen table. She used the towel to apply firm pressure to the wound.

"Hold this," she ordered him.

"I'm fine," he grumbled, his voice gruff. "Just tired."

"We still need to stop the bleeding. Hold it."

As soon as he was holding it in place, she picked up the cordless phone from the counter to call 911. A baby's wail cut across the silence before she could dial.

"Here." Lieutenant Willis held out his left hand, keeping his right pressed firmly against the towel. "I will call. You take care of the baby."

Maggie narrowed her eyes at him. Could she trust him enough to turn her back on him while she tended to her babies? A second loud bellow decided for her. Her daughter had no volume control. Maggie knew from experience that the baby girl would only get louder until her needs were met. Nodding, she thrust the phone into his outstretched hand and hurried across the room to the stroller, where the babies still sat. Rory was still asleep, his head slumped against one side of the stroller. Siobhan was a different story. She continued wailing until Maggie picked her up. Then she was all smiles as one chubby hand tangled itself in Maggie's curls and the other waved in the air while she babbled. Maggie went to the refrigerator and prepared a sippy cup of milk under the malevolent stare of the attacker.

Someone knocked on the back door. Maggie shrieked and dropped the cup, clasping her daughter protectively against her. Cold milk sloshed on her faded jeans. The child squawked in protest.

"Police," a voice called out.

"In here," Lieutenant Willis responded.

A pair of uniformed policemen stepped into the room. One of them glanced over at Maggie, still holding her squirming, fussing daughter, milk dripping on the floor.

"Sorry, ma'am. Didn't mean to startle you."

Not sure she would be able to speak, Maggie nodded and bent down to retrieve the cup. Keeping a wary eye on the visitors in her small kitchen, she poured her daughter another cup and handed it to her. Knowing Siobhan would be occupied for a few minutes, she set her daughter down on the rug behind her. Happy, the child slurped her milk while Maggie used the towel hanging on the refrigerator door to clean up the mess.

"You guys got here quick," Lieutenant Willis noted, a wry twist to his lips. "I only called five minutes ago."

"Yes, sir. We were on our way back from another call a mile from here."

The lieutenant nodded once. "Very good, gentlemen. You can take this guy off my hands." He jerked his head toward the sneering man sitting on the floor.

The officers hefted the handcuffed man to his feet and led him toward the door.

"You okay, Lieutenant? Need us to call the paramedics?"

Dan waved a dismissive hand at them. "Done. I think the bleeding's stopped, anyway."

"Read him his rights yet?"

"Yep. He's all yours. Get him a nice, cozy cell."

The man jeered at them. "You guys think you're so tough." He shot a snide glance at Maggie. "And you—don't think this is the end. He knows where you live now. And even if you move…it'll be easy to track you down with *them*." He motioned with his head toward the little girl, who had abandoned her cup and was crawling away. Maggie grabbed the child, ignoring her squawk of protest. Her stomach curdled, ached, and her mouth grew dry.

The officers nudged the man toward the door. "Dude, you have the right to remain silent. I'd seriously consider doing that."

Lieutenant Willis stood abruptly. He put a hand on the lead officer's shoulder, halting him so he could stare down the attacker.

Maggie shivered. Wow, his gray eyes were so cold. And hard. With his longer-than-regulation-length blond hair and leather jacket, he looked carefree. But she had seen him in action. This was not a man to be messed with. Not to mention the fact that he had to be at least six feet tall. Six feet of muscle.

"Who is after her?" Even though his voice was soft, Maggie could clearly hear it across the room.

The man raised his chin defiantly. "I got my rights. I want a lawyer. And a phone call."

Lieutenant Willis's expression melted into a scowl. He jerked his head toward the door. "Get him outta here."

The officers dragged the man from the house. Lieutenant Willis sat heavily, a sigh escaping as he stared at Maggie. He was gearing up to ask questions. Lots of questions. She could almost imagine his thoughts aligning themselves in his head. Her spine straightened. Just because she didn't have a choice about talking to him didn't mean she had to like it. But he had saved her—and her babies. She had no doubt her attacker would have hurt them, too, to try to get answers out of her. The lieutenant's rescue had to mean something. She would cooperate. But still, she'd better keep up her guard.

The arrival of the paramedics forestalled the interrogation. The stoic lieutenant made a big show of tossing the bloody towel over his shoulder to allow the men to examine him. The bleeding had stopped. It was soon clear that he hadn't been stabbed as much as sliced, the blade grazing his skin in a shallow cut. He wouldn't even require stitches. Although he wasn't badly hurt, she could see fatigue settling deep in the lines on his face.

Too soon for her comfort, the paramedics had packed up their things and departed. Now it was just her and the lieutenant. *Here come the questions*, she thought, resigned. But she was surprised.

"See-ob-han?" the man queried, head tilted while he peered at the blanket she had tucked around her daughter, now sleeping peacefully against her shoulder. Maggie glanced down. It was the blanket Wendy had given her right before she'd left. Maggie had been so touched when the woman had made one for each twin, their names embroidered on the front.

"It's pronounced She-vonne," she corrected him. "It's Irish."

"Ah, that's right. Your mother is from Ireland."

Maggie shrugged, not prepared to discuss her mother with this stranger. Even if he had saved her life.

"Are you taking it easy on the job, Willis?"

Lieutenant Willis snapped to attention as a petite officer entered the room. Her short graying mop of hair was slightly wavy and curled under at the ends. She carried herself with authority. Maggie could almost feel the energy crackling from her as she walked.

Maggie edged over to the stroller and set her sleeping daughter inside it, never taking her eyes off the new arrival.

"No, ma'am. Just starting to ask Maggie here why someone would come after her with a knife."

"That's a good question, Lieutenant." The woman's brown eyes zeroed in on Maggie. They were eyes used to smiling, surrounded by laugh lines. But right now they were stern. "I'm Chief Martha Garraway from the local precinct. I'm very interested in your answer, Ms. Slade. We've looked for you a long time. Used valuable resources to find you. It's apparent someone else was looking, too. Any idea who?"

Maggie drew in a fortifying breath. She was in deep. If it had been only herself, she would have run for it. But she had to think of her children. They needed to be protected.

"I know exactly who it was. It was the man who killed my husband."

TWO

"**Y**our husband!" Lieutenant Willis blurted.

Maggie swiveled her head from Lieutenant Willis to Chief Garraway, her brow furrowed. Her lips pressed together as she studied the thunderstruck expressions on their faces. Well, they apparently hadn't expected that to come out of her mouth.

"How could you not know that I was married if you have been searching for me?" Maggie planted her fists firmly on her hips, shaking her head at them. Seriously? "Wasn't that why you wanted to find me, because I disappeared after my husband was murdered?"

Lieutenant Willis scowled, his gray eyes narrowed. But he made no answer.

"Okay, Ms. Slade... Is it Ms. Slade?" Chief Garraway's smooth voice was the epitome of politeness. Her stiff posture and frosty gaze, however, flashed a clear warning that she wasn't pleased. This was not a woman who enjoyed looking foolish.

Still, Maggie hesitated. She had developed a strong distrust of cops since Phillip's murder. Her mind screamed at her to be careful. Don't give too much away. Then she shot a glance at Lieutenant Willis. Her eyes caught on the bloody towel still draped across his shoulder and her heart clenched. He had taken that knife wound for her. Would he have put himself in harm's way to protect her if he were on her enemy's side? Her glance flicked back to the towel, then to his wounded side. Although the wound was hidden, she could see that he was holding himself stiffly. She recalled that he had refused to be medicated, despite being in pain. He'd told the paramedics that he needed to stay alert, to stand guard over her and her children. That decided it for her. She would trust them…to a point. She wouldn't reveal everything. Not until she knew for sure she could trust them.

"I kept my maiden name, so yes, my last name is still Slade." Let them think what they wanted about that.

Chief Garraway nodded. "Okay. Ms. Slade, we have gone over your history with a fine-tooth comb. There is no evidence that you were recently married. Or that you have ever been married."

Maggie threw her hands in the air. She whirled and paced to the window. Still cautious, she remained to the side of the curtained panes and glanced beneath the blinds. When she was calm enough to speak, she pivoted and fused her gaze with the chief's. "We married in Las Vegas, on a whim. We filed for a license and then went to a chapel. There's no waiting in Vegas."

"Las Vegas? You mean like Elvis? Why would you do that?" Her hackles rose at the poorly disguised scorn in Lieutenant Willis's voice.

"Yes, Las Vegas. What's wrong with that?" Maggie tossed her head. How dare that man judge her? "Lots of people get married there. It's completely legal."

She wanted to wince at the petulance she heard in her own voice. She should stop talking. She didn't need to explain her actions to him. But for some reason his scorn really got to her.

"I don't care about why you got married in Las Vegas," the chief asserted, throwing a silencing glare at her lieutenant. "You could have gone to the moon for all I care. But there should have been some trace of a marriage license in your records. And I'm also concerned that you are claiming to have witnessed a murder, yet you never came forward. I need to understand why. It's obvious you're in danger. Were you somehow involved in whatever happened to your husband? Is that why someone is after you now, why you were in hiding?"

Was she a suspect? Maggie's eyes widened, and her breath hitched in alarm. Never once had she dreamed that she could be facing charges. She found it ironic that after being a juror who had convicted a woman six years ago for murder, she could face jail time for a similar crime. She shuddered.

"I haven't done anything wrong! I was running for my life!"

"Relax. We're just trying to figure this out. You have to admit, your actions are suspicious."

Maggie whirled to face the tall lieutenant, who was even now observing her, his eyes narrowed. His mouth was a hard line slashed across his handsome face. "I had nothing to do with his murder..." She stopped. What if it *had* been her fault? She had wondered that often during the past eighteen months.

"Something tells me you're not sure of that."

Maggie stared at him, a wave of helplessness pounding into her. Rory dropped his pacifier and startled, whimpering as he awoke.

"Maggie, why don't you get your children settled.

Then we will talk. But I warn you, I expect you to tell me everything."

She was cornered. In her own living room. It was too bad she and God weren't on speaking terms. She could really use someone in her corner about now.

With a stiff nod, she turned away from the officers invading her home and went to get Rory and Siobhan settled in their cribs. Fortunately, they both were exhausted and settled down to sleep without fuss. For several minutes, she stood over them, her chest tight as she fought to control her anxiety. Whatever happened, she couldn't go to jail. What would happen to them? Foster care? Maybe they'd even be separated.

A shadow blocked out the hallway light briefly before moving aside. Startled, she looked up. Lieutenant Willis stood in the doorway. His expressionless face gave no clue as to what he was thinking.

"Are you about ready?" His cool tone hit her like a whip. She straightened her spine and moved toward him, pausing until he stepped aside to allow her to precede him. Chief Garraway was on her cell phone pacing in front of the kitchen door while she listened to the person on the other end. She held up her finger as she spotted them. Maggie walked to the love seat and dropped down. She pulled her legs up onto the seat and hugged her knees to her chest, resting her chin against them.

"I want to know as soon as his lawyer arrives. We need to get this situation under control…Sounds good." Covering the mouthpiece of the phone, she whispered to Lieutenant Willis, "The perp is waiting for his lawyer. Hopefully he will turn on whoever hired him."

The love seat shifted slightly as Lieutenant Willis lowered himself down beside her. She shifted closer to her side as inconspicuously as she could. Considering the way he smirked at her, she wasn't very successful. She forgot about her discomfort with his nearness as he rubbed his side, grimacing.

"Are you okay, Lieutenant?" she whispered, casting a glance at the chief, who wasn't paying any attention to them. "I could get you some ice or a heating pad. I'm not really sure which would be better."

He sighed. "I'm fine. I've had worse."

Which of course meant he didn't want her to fuss over him. She rolled her eyes. "Men."

"What do you mean, men?"

"Get a knife wound, and it's nothing. Get a cold, and the world ends."

"That's not true."

"Yeah, it is. My husband was all macho, but when he got a cold, he wanted to be babied. He was a horrible patient."

"Speaking of your husband, it's time we talked about what happened to him."

Maggie jumped. She didn't feel bad as she noticed the lieutenant did, too. Obviously, he wasn't in top form. He apparently hadn't noticed his commanding officer approaching them, either.

She shook her head. She just needed to get through this. Drawing a deep lungful of air to steel herself, Maggie turned to face the chief. Surprisingly, though, it was the lieutenant who spoke.

"The last information we have on you is that you started working at the *LaMar Pond Journal* as a fact-checker three years ago. About two years ago, you made an appointment to come talk with the police. You never kept that appointment. You sent an email stating you needed to reschedule. But you never did."

Maggie blinked. Nodded. "Yes. I remember. I had forgotten about that."

The man beside her sat forward, his expression intent. "I didn't. I was the cop you made the appointment with. Until someone spotted you and called the missing persons hotline, I was looking for a body."

It was petty, but there was some satisfaction in watching the shock widen her eyes. He hadn't been joking. He had been sure she was dead.

"Why would you assume I was dead?" He hadn't noticed the soft lilt in her voice before, just the softest touch of an Irish accent.

"Remember that case, the trial for Melanie Swanson?" He waited for her nod before continuing. "It turned out several of the jurors had been threatened to give a guilty verdict. Melanie was framed, and the real killers wanted to cover their tracks. A few of the blackmailed jurors eventually tried to come forward to tell the truth, and they were murdered. I thought you had been, too."

He had a hollow feeling inside as he remembered thinking he had allowed one more life to slip through his hands.

"Wait…she was innocent? That girl accused of murder? Oh, I feel awful! I thought she did it." Her hands covered her face. Her entire posture suggested she was blaming herself for not seeing the truth. Dan could empathize; he knew only too well how it felt to have your insides torn out by guilt. By the feeling that you hadn't done enough, hadn't tried hard enough.

"Don't. Feel guilty, I mean. You did your duty. If you really thought she committed the crime, then you had to vote that way."

"If you didn't make an appointment with the police because of the trial, then why had you made the appointment?" Chief Garraway had stationed herself directly in front of Maggie, a position that said she was in control. Normally, Dan would have remained standing, too. At the moment, though, he couldn't seem to find the energy to rise. Between spending the past week on the late shift, hunting down Maggie and now getting stabbed, he was whupped good.

Some hair was hanging in his face, annoying him. Shaking it back out of his eyes, he focused on Maggie as she answered.

"I had thought that I was being followed. But almost as soon as I made the appointment, it stopped. I canceled the appointment. I'm sorry. I should have called you in person to tell you why, but I was embarrassed. Then I got married, and I forgot about it…until Phillip was killed."

"Back to Phillip. Tell me about him."

The chief's tone made it clear this wasn't a request.

Shrugging her shoulders, Maggie's eyes grew distant. Dan could practically see the thoughts whirling in her head as she searched for where to begin. He could see her pain weighing her down as she remembered.

Dan watched the woman with a clinical sort of interest. She was beautiful, he acknowledged—but that wasn't what interested him right now. What he found interesting was the tenseness in her posture. Everything about her suggested the willingness to run at a moment's notice. He had the feeling that the only things that were keeping her in that house at that moment were the two children sleeping in the next room. Somehow he felt that they were the only things that anchored her to anything. He had seen that same sort of wariness in soldiers' eyes in the battlefield in Afghanistan. Was it just the trauma of seeing her husband killed before her eyes? If indeed there had been a husband. He still felt the need to see some proof of that. Growing up in the foster care system had taught him that there were many people willing to play on others' sympathy to get what they wanted.

But deep inside, he believed her, although he couldn't say why.

Just as he was beginning to think that the silence had gone on for too long, Maggie appeared to come to some sort of decision. She nodded her head, lifted her chin and faced them with defiance beaming out of her eyes. The most incredible blue eyes he could ever remember seeing. Where on earth had that thought come from?

"His full name was Phillip Michael Nelson," she began. Although she appeared calm, he detected a slight tremor in her voice. "We met about three years ago, right after I started working at the *Journal*. We got engaged a year later. We never really got around to planning a wedding or setting a date. Then one day, Phillip said he had it all figured out, and that we should rush off to Las Vegas to get married."

"And you just went along with that?" Dan blurted out. He didn't mean to sound so incredulous, but man, he just couldn't picture it. How could an intelligent woman not ask the important questions? Questions such as "Hey, honey, why the hurry?" They'd already waited a year.

"Why wouldn't I?" Maggie snapped. "I trusted him. If it meant that much to him, I was fine with it."

Chief Garraway gave Dan a stern look that clearly told him to keep his opinions to himself. Dan grimaced. Normally he had iron control over his emotions, but right now he was tired and in pain. Not to mention something about Maggie really confused him. He wasn't used to feeling off balance. He sighed and nodded at the chief to show her that he had gotten the message.

Pulling his phone from his pocket, he sent a quick text to Jace with Phillip's name. This process would move quicker if he had the case details. A minute later, his phone vibrated. He read the text and frowned.

"This just keeps getting stranger," he muttered to himself.

"Lieutenant?"

He shook his head and handed Chief Garraway his phone. "I had Lieutenant Tucker check our case files. No Phillip Michael Nelson was ever reported as dead or missing in LaMar Pond."

Chief Garraway narrowed her eyes as she read the message for herself. Her lips pressed together. "Ms. Slade," she said finally, "do you happen to have a picture of your husband?"

Maggie sprang to her feet and dashed out of the room. The sound of a drawer opening and closing came through the thin walls. A moment later, she hurried back, holding a small photo album in her hand. She flipped through it as she approached until she found the picture she wanted. Then she handed it to the chief, who in turn glanced at the photo and handed it to Dan.

"Yeah, I remember him. We found him in Lake Erie. He had been shot. We were never able to identify him."

He hesitated. If he had been alone with the chief, he'd be fine giving her the rest of the information. He decided to hold his tongue until he could get the chief by herself.

"You found him in the lake?" Maggie whispered, her voice cracking, pain saturating each word.

She covered her face with both hands briefly, shuddering. A strange tension seized him. *Not tears. Please, Lord, anything but tears.* He was relieved when she brought her hands away from her face. Her lashes were damp, but no tears fell.

"I don't understand. He was killed in our house."

That surprised him. "In your house? We went through your house after you disappeared. There was no sign of murder."

"Not that house. The one we were fixing up together."

"We found no other property in your name."

Maggie rolled her eyes and sighed. "That's because it's not in my name. It's in my mother's name. She was selling it to us. But the deal hadn't closed yet."

Chief Garraway nodded. "Okay. Just tell us what happened."

Maggie took a deep breath. "I came home from work early and heard arguing. It was really loud. I walked to the doorway of the kitchen. Phillip saw me and shouted for me to run. He threw himself at the other man. The gun went off and Phillip fell. I ran out, hopped in my car and took off."

"Why didn't you go to the police, Ms. Slade?" Chief Garraway inquired.

"Because the man who shot him was dressed as a policeman."

Silence.

"Let me get this straight, a cop killed your husband?"

Dread curled in Dan's stomach. It felt as though he'd eaten a lead ball for lunch. *Not again*, he thought wildly. As much as he didn't want to believe her, didn't want to believe that someone charged to serve and protect could do the opposite, he had seen that happen too often in the past. If there was even the possibility, it needed to be taken seriously.

Apparently, Maggie thought he was mocking her. She burst to her feet and crossed her arms across her chest. "I'm not lying! He was dressed like a cop! He kept demanding that Phillip hand something over. He threatened to bring him into the station. Said the chief of police had issued a warrant for his arrest."

"You said the man demanded Nelson hand something over. Any idea what it was?" Now they were getting somewhere.

But she shook her head and sank wearily back onto the couch. "I don't know. I had to get out of there. The man might have said he wanted to arrest Phillip, but he wasn't holding handcuffs, he was holding his gun— and he looked like he couldn't wait to use it. I think he planned to kill Phillip all along. And then I realized he would know who I was. I'd brought over plenty of my things—letters and paperwork with my name on them—and there were pictures of Phillip and me together on our wedding day hanging on the wall. It wouldn't be hard for him to know who I was."

Chief Garraway turned back to Dan. "What information was the LaMar PD able to find out about Nelson after he was found?"

Dan shook his head. "Not much, Chief. His fingerprints weren't in any databases, so he had no criminal record."

"Did you circulate his picture?"

"Yes, ma'am. But it must have set off some sort of red flag. Before we got any responses, the FBI stepped in and took over. We were out of the whole case."

"The FBI?" Chief Garraway's voice rose in surprise. "Just what was your husband involved with, Ms. Slade?"

"Chief, I can have the LaMar department go over to Maggie's other house and see if they can find anything." When she nodded, he got the address from Maggie and stepped outside to call Paul. A few minutes later, he hung up. More bad news. He sighed and pivoted on his heel to head back inside. Stopped.

A row of high shrubs blocked the side of the house from the street. But from his angle, Dan could clearly make out several sets of footprints in the dirt between the house and the shrubs. They had to have been recent, since it had just rained two days ago. The sizes were different, showing that they belonged to more than one person, but all of them were large footprints. Much too large to have been Maggie's.

He burst inside, startling the women. Briskly, he explained what he had seen.

"That means that you were being watched. Probably to determine your identity. And by more than one man. Whoever that man sitting in jail is, he had a partner. Maybe the man who killed your husband. Maybe someone else. We have no way of knowing how many people are involved."

Chief Garraway took charge. "Right. Willis, request officers to process the scene. Ms. Slade and her children will accompany us to the station. This house is not safe for them, even with us here."

Dan remembered his conversation with Paul. As

hesitant as he was to deliver more bad news, there was no sense in holding back. "I checked with the LaMar Pond PD. The address that Maggie gave me burned down eighteen months ago."

THREE

What had her husband been involved with? The question reverberated around Maggie's brain time and time again as she rushed about getting herself and the twins ready to go. Maggie got herself and her cranky kids out the door in record time. The idea that someone had been watching her gave her the willies.

Not to mention the obvious fact that somebody had tried to kill her earlier. This house was no longer safe for her. Or her babies. She glanced over at the lieutenant just in time to see him wince and rub his side. She grimaced, feeling guilty that he had been injured while protecting her. With her hair tucked inside a hat, Maggie followed the cops out to the cars. With reluctance, she watched her babies being belted into their car seats in the chief's car. Lieutenant Willis straightened up, sketched a cocky salute at the chief and sauntered to his own car on the street. She definitely would have preferred to ride with the lieutenant rather than his stern-faced chief. But she went where her children went, so she stepped into the car without protest and buckled up.

"I don't suppose it would be possible to let the owner

know no one is in her house?" Wendy had been a good friend. She hated to let her down.

"We can do that. Will she shorten her mission trip?" Realizing her mouth had fallen open, Maggie closed it with a click. They really had researched everything.

"Either that or she'll have to find someone else to house-sit."

"Good." Chief Garraway touched her radio. "Move out, Lieutenant. We don't have all day."

Lieutenant Willis's voice responded back with a pert "You got it."

Almost as soon as they merged onto the interstate, Siobhan started to fuss. Maggie looked at the chief, expecting to see an impatient frown. Instead, she saw the other woman's lips twitch.

She blinked, sure she had imagined it. Nope. Chief Garraway's mouth had turned up at the corners. Amazing.

"It never fails, does it?" The chief's voice was mild, conversational. "They can be as quiet as mice, but the moment you are trapped in a car with them, they start wailing. At least that was my experience with my own."

Maggie had no idea how she was supposed to respond to that. It had never occurred to her that Chief Garraway might be a wife and mother. The older woman wore her authority like a cloak. It was hard to look past it.

"I'm going to see if she will calm down with a pacifier." Maggie twisted in her seat to place a pacifier in her daughter's mouth. As she did so, she noticed a car moving toward them. It was dodging in and out of the traffic. Unease slithered down her spine and sank into her stomach, leaving a greasy, queasy feeling.

"Chief," she began, her voice pitched low so as not to further disturb the babies.

"I see him." She touched the button to the radio. "Lieutenant? We have a vehicle that appears to be moving in on us."

"I'm a little ways behind you, Chief. I will—"

They never heard what he was going to do. The car was beside them. It jackknifed, slamming into the chief's car's side. She yelled as the driver's door caved in and her left arm slammed against the window. It remained limply at her side as she continued to steer with her right hand. In the backseat, the twins started screaming in terror. Desperate to see her babies and ascertain if they were hurt, Maggie started to unbuckle.

"Don't you dare!" the chief barked.

Realizing how her being unbuckled could affect the chief's driving, Maggie clenched her fists and remained seated. Her jaw started to ache. She had started grinding her teeth.

A siren blared as Lieutenant Willis roared up behind their attacker, a blue light flashing on the dashboard of his unmarked car.

The other vehicle sped away, zigzagging furiously through the traffic. Lieutenant Willis pursued the car, but Maggie could see the distance between the cars growing. His voice came over the radio, snapping out a description of the car, its license plate and location. Maggie could almost feel his frustration crackling through the radio.

"Lost him, Chief." They could barely hear his voice over the howling twins.

"Understood, Lieutenant. We are pulling off. Need to have the babies checked over."

Chief Garraway maneuvered the cruiser awkwardly off the next ramp, calling for an ambulance crew as she did so. Her face was drawn with pain, and sweat was beading on her forehead.

The car had barely stopped moving when Maggie pushed open the door and ran to the back door. After wrenching it open, she checked on the twins. Only the chief's demand that she not remove the children from their seats or the vehicle prevented her from grabbing her babies out of the car. Worry simmered in her gut as she tried to soothe the angry twins. A couple of times she winced as Siobhan hit a piercing note.

When the ambulance crew arrived, it soon became apparent that the chief was stuck inside the vehicle. Maggie's heart bled for Chief Garraway. The older woman was obviously in pain, wincing and muffling groans. Maggie couldn't help but feel that this situation was somehow her fault. *Stop it! You didn't ask for any of this.* Still, the knowledge that within twenty-four hours two officers had been injured trying to protect her was humbling. Maggie felt the weight of the debt she owed them. She grimaced. She didn't like being in debt to anyone.

Two members of the crew used a set of metal cutters and set about the arduous task of extracting the chief from the damaged vehicle. The noise was horrendous. While they were doing that, another team member carefully examined Rory, Siobhan and Maggie. Lieutenant Willis pulled in as the crew was strapping Chief Garraway onto a stretcher. He leaped from his car and hurried over to his chief, an anxious expression on his face. Even injured, the woman was reluctant to hand over control.

"This is an attempted murder investigation here, Lieutenant. But we need to know what happened back in LaMar Pond that started all of this. She's the only one who can identify the man who shot her husband. Do what you can to uncover the truth at that end. She's the key to all of this. If our department can help you in any way, just ask."

"Yes, ma'am. I'll take care of it."

"Your children seem to be fine, miss." Maggie turned her attention to the young paramedic who was looking over Rory. The baby boy had stopped fussing now that he had been removed from the terrifying vehicle and had a full view of his mother. He smiled and waved his chubby arms at her. Overwhelmed with relief, Maggie's eyes burned as tears gathered. She blinked them away, although one managed to escape down her cheek. The paramedic handed Rory to her, and she cuddled him close. When he protested and squirmed, she realized she was gripping him too close. She had almost lost them. These children were the only things that mattered in her life. She had to do everything she could to protect them.

"Mama! Mama!" Siobhan demanded her attention. Maggie bent down and made what she called the twin exchange. Rory stopped fussing as soon as he was free.

Siobhan was another story.

Dan stepped back from the ambulance as the driver closed the door, effectively cutting off his view of Chief Garraway. It was rather shocking to see the indomitable chief put out of commission. As far back as he could remember, she had never even taken a sick day. And here she was being wheeled away in an ambulance.

The sniffling noises behind him reminded him of

the reason why his former chief was injured. Maggie was comforting Siobhan, bouncing the disgruntled little girl on her hip and shushing her. It wasn't fair, but he felt an irrational surge of anger toward the woman. If it hadn't been for her, Chief Garraway would be fine. All because she'd been too chicken to go to the police a year and a half earlier. *If she was telling the truth about the corrupt cop, going to the police might have caused her to be killed herself.*

Enough. He had a job to do.

"Can you get her settled down enough to move to my car?"

Maggie jerked up her head, startled.

"You're not supposed to reuse car seats that have been in accidents," she gasped. "They might be defective."

He sighed impatiently and rolled his neck on his shoulders. This day had been too long already.

"Look, Maggie, right now I'm more worried about the jerk that has it out for you. Defective car seats are better than none at all. You and your kiddos are targets here. We need to move. Now."

Maggie hesitated, then nodded. She handed Siobhan to him. Startled, he grabbed for the little girl. Sweat broke out on his forehead. He had never held a baby before. What if he dropped her? What if…? Siobhan trained huge blue eyes on his face and stared. Oh, no. What if she started screaming? But she didn't scream. She grinned, then laughed. Her chubby hands found his beard and pulled. Hard.

Dan winced.

"Vonnie," Maggie cooed near his ear, deftly reaching out her free hand to disentangle her daughter. "Don't touch his beard, sweetie. Who knows when he last washed it?"

Dan swung his head around to glare and encountered her mischief-filled blue eyes.

"Huh. Your kids have your eyes." Well, now that was a dumb thing to say.

She blushed. She sure was cute when she got flustered.

Focus, man. Focus. You don't need to start thinking about women. They're pure poison to you. Too many things go wrong when women and children get involved.

He turned on his heel and led the way to his waiting vehicle. As soon as the seats were set up and the kids were buckled in, he started driving. A couple exits down, he turned off and headed north.

"Where are we going, Lieutenant Willis?" Maggie asked, her voice tense and worried. He remembered that she had a distrust of police officers. "The police station isn't this way. I drive past it every week when I go shopping."

"I know. My priority right now is the safety of you and your children. And that means I need to find out what happened to your husband. The good thing is that I'm not actually with Garraway's unit anymore, so I don't need to stick around while they investigate at this end." He glanced at her. The anxious look on her face had faded, and she looked thoughtful instead. "And I'm thinking we need to stay under the radar for a while. Which means you should probably call me Dan instead of Lieutenant."

She gave him a pointed look. "I noticed that you never call me Ms. Slade like Chief Garraway. You always call me Maggie. As if we know each other."

A wave of heat flooded his face. He hadn't realized

he had been doing that. "Sorry. I've been looking for you for a long time. In LaMar Pond, we got used to referring to you as Maggie. It stuck. I meant no offense."

A feminine shrug answered him. "I'm not offended. I just was surprised at how casual you were."

Dan nodded but didn't speak. His mind was busy with a problem. He was positive that Phillip Nelson's murder, the arson on the house and the attack on Maggie were all linked. Which meant someone was out to get her. Probably because of whatever it was that they had wanted from Phillip. That raised several urgent questions.

What had Phillip gotten himself into? Who was after Maggie? And how was he supposed to keep her low profile if she was conspicuously traveling around with twins? Not that the kids weren't adorable. He sneaked a glance in the rearview mirror. They were facing backward. All he could make out were Rory's feet as he kicked them in the air. A smile tugged at his mouth. He tried to keep it down. He needed to come up with a solution.

"Hold on." He pulled to the side of the road. The driver of the car behind him swerved to miss him and blared his horn.

"Should have followed the two-second rule, buddy," he muttered.

"Hey, watch how you drive, Dan! You have kids in the car." Maggie glared at him.

"Yeah, sorry." Dan pulled out his cell phone and shot off a quick message to Paul. He had an idea, but he needed the LaMar Pond chief to handle the logistics.

Paul sent a message back a minute later. Satisfied, Dan flipped on his blinker and slipped back into traffic.

"Is everything all right?"

Maggie looked tense again, her hands clenching and unclenching in her lap.

"Just solving a problem. Nothing you need to worry about."

Unfortunately, her expression darkened. She bit her lip, hard. He winced, half expecting her to draw blood. Obviously, his words weren't reassuring.

"Honestly, Maggie, it's nothing. I just had a question, so I texted my chief."

"Chief Garraway is on the way to the hospital." Maggie furrowed her brow and tilted her head. The corners of her mouth turned down in a slight frown.

"Not Garraway. Chief Kennedy. In LaMar Pond. He's my official boss now."

At the words *LaMar Pond*, the blood drained from Maggie's face. Her eyes grew huge in her face. She clenched her hands together so tightly that her knuckles whitened. The air almost vibrated with her fear.

"LaMar Pond? I can't go back there! I just can't!" A slight edge of hysteria shadowed her words.

Dan reached over and set his hand over her clenched fists. He took his eyes off the road long enough to look into her eyes. Seeing that she was in control again, he removed his hand and returned his eyes to the road.

"I know you are scared." He kept his voice low, just a soft rumble in the strained silence. "I don't blame you. But for your safety, and for your kids' safety, we have to find out who is after you. And what secret is in your husband's past."

Sneaking a peek over, he saw that Maggie looked far from convinced. Her face was still pale, and he could detect a tremble in her hands, which she tried to hide as soon as she noticed him looking at them. Not much he could do about that. Whether she trusted him or not, he had a job to do. And to his way of thinking, the sooner this particular job was done, the better.

He saw a sign for the next gas station. It was sheer reflex to check the fuel gauge. Oh, man, they were getting pretty low. They would have to stop.

"What are we doing?" Maggie asked as he pulled off at the exit ramp.

"We have to get gas." He pulled into the station, carefully watching out the windows for any sign of pursuit before he opened the door. The chain gas station was equipped with a food mart. Dan could see nothing but trees and hills behind them, although there were houses down the road a bit. Maggie threw open the other door, but he grabbed her arm before she could exit.

"You should stay in the car," he said. "It's safer."

"I should change the twins' diapers," she argued. "Can't you smell it?"

Dan took a deep whiff and wished he hadn't. Okay, so she had a point. He let go of her arm, and she rushed out of the car and to the backseat. He listened with half an ear for squalling and was shocked when there was none. Huh. Guess the kids were going to cooperate. With an efficiency born of the urgent situation, he filled the gas tank, tapping his fist impatiently on the roof until it was done. He grabbed his receipt from the machine.

Maggie had the twins unbuckled as she hurried to finish up changing their diapers.

"If we hurry, could we go in and grab some milk and snack items?" she asked. "It's going to be a long ride. The kids will get hungry."

Dan kept his eyes scouring the road in front of them. He really didn't like sitting out in the open like this. But he trusted Maggie to know what was best for her kids.

"Okay." He squinted at Maggie. She had the serviceable backpack she used as a diaper bag slung across her back. He'd never thought of it, but it was probably hard to carry a diaper bag with a wiggling kid in each arm. By unspoken agreement they each bent down on their side to grab a kid.

Smash!

The window shattered as a bullet hit it. Two inches from Maggie's head.

FOUR

Maggie screamed and pulled a shrieking Rory from the car.

"Run!" Dan bellowed. She needed no further urging. With a runner's sprint, she hurtled toward the trees. Dan was on her heels, cradling Siobhan tightly in his arms.

A car screeched into the parking lot, bullets spewing from the open window. The ground was pelted ruthlessly, dust flying. It looked like the same car that had crashed into the chief's.

Dan looked back in time to see a bullet hit a gas pump.

"Faster!" he barked. Ducking his head, he forced himself to hold the baby tighter and push forward.

The pump exploded. A nanosecond later, the flames set off a second pump. Dan yelled as the back of his leather jacket ignited. "Take her!"

Maggie grabbed the baby and Dan dived for the ground, rolling until the flames were out. He thanked God with all his heart that his jacket had taken the worst of the fire. He had, however, twisted his knee when he'd dived to the ground. Forcing himself to stand, he limped next to Maggie. He had never seen anything more beautiful than her tired face, scratched by broken glass but otherwise uninjured. And the babies. Wailing. Fat tears dribbled down their faces. But they were alive. He hadn't let them down. Not like before...

Remembering the car, he looked over his shoulder. Both his car and the attacker's were smoldering chunks of charred metal. He started toward the destruction, then halted, his cop radar on full alert. Another vehicle was approaching from the other direction, slowing down. He pulled Maggie and the twins farther out of sight.

"Trees. Get to the trees," he gritted, taking Siobhan from her arms. Maggie looked as if she might protest, but he scowled at her. He wasn't about to let an injury keep him from doing his duty. He would protect them, no matter the personal cost.

"Your back..."

"Is fine. My leg twisted. I'll live. Move!"

She didn't argue. They moved as quickly as his injured leg would allow. Once they were hidden, they slowed long enough to confirm Dan's suspicions. The car had stopped, and two men had stepped out, carrying guns. They ignored the assailant's car but inspected Dan's still-burning car from a distance, bending to peer inside. Dan was too far away to hear what was said, but as the men started to look around the perimeter of the gas station, Dan urged Maggie farther back into the trees. It was only a matter of time before the men started to expand the search for Maggie and Dan.

"In the zippered front pocket of my backpack, you'll find a baggie with pacifiers. Can you get it?" Maggie turned so Dan could reach out and open the pocket with one hand. Grabbing the baggie, he held it out to her. She grabbed the pacifiers and plopped one in each child's mouth. Ah, silence.

Muttering a prayer of thanksgiving that they were alive, Dan prayed for their continued safety. And that Rory and Siobhan wouldn't start crying again and give them away. Especially Siobhan, who was the loudest child he had ever heard. Unthinking, he kissed the baby's head in silent apology for his unkind thoughts. Then he swung his gaze to Maggie, hoping she had missed the action. The eyes that met his were exhausted, but he saw the smile tugging at her lips. Oops. Busted.

He led the way farther into the woods, stopping several times to listen. The third time he stopped, he caught the distinctive sound of male voices coming from where they had been. Urgency filled him as he picked up the pace, changing directions and heading in a zigzag pattern through the woods. God had heard his prayer, he noticed in relief. Both Rory and Siobhan remained quiet.

The voices died away. The men had headed in the other direction. Dan continued to push his little group through the wooded area. Several times, he glanced at his phone. No bars. Figured. Pennsylvania's hills were breathtaking, but they wreaked havoc with modern technology. He continued walking until he finally had a single bar. He passed Siobhan to Maggie, then motioned for her to keep back. He stepped several feet away from them, his nerves stretched tight as he drew closer to where the trees ended. Close by, the whir of traffic let him know that they were near a road. Using the GPS on his phone, he pinpointed their location.

How were the bad guys finding them? Were they following him? The idea seemed impossible, but he couldn't see any other way that they could have pinned them down so quickly. Well, if some kind of tracker was in the car, it was gone. Quickly, he removed the battery from his phone and checked it for bugs. Nothing. He reassembled the phone.

It had to have been the car. Someone must have planted a tracker on it while he'd been inside Maggie's house talking to her and Chief Garraway. Or it could have even happened earlier, before he left LaMar Pond. Was Phillip's killer still there, still connected to the police department? Dan had put the call on speaker when that woman said she had found Maggie. Anyone in the station could have overheard, realized Dan would go to check out the lead and sneaked something onto his car before he left.

A quick glance over his shoulder assured him that the children and Maggie were fine. He ignored the tugging at his heart at the sight of the woebegone little family. Bitterness rose like bile in him at the thought of the family he would never have himself. What woman would want a man with his issues, his past? What kind of father could he possibly be?

Deliberately, he closed his mind to the dreams he'd had before the war had destroyed them. He sent a quick text to the police department, outlining his situation and his present location. In record time, he received an answer. Satisfied, he nodded to himself. Then he shot off a text to Paul, warning him to search for bugs or other surveillance equipment that might have gone missing.

Returning to the others, he kept his eyes peeled, constantly searching for movement in the line of trees behind them. He kept his voice low, cautious.

"Maggie, we need to keep moving. The department is sending us an unmarked car with enough provisions to get us through the next day or so if need be. Problem is, we're going to have to walk a little ways yet to get to the drop-off spot."

He focused his concerned gaze on her weary, dirt-smeared face. The twins were starting to get fractious. Rory had his fist in his mouth, gnawing on it. Siobhan was whimpering. Dan was worried. For a child as vocal as she usually was, did whimpering mean something was truly wrong? More than the situation at hand, that was?

A wan smile flitted across Maggie's face. She nodded, then pulled the backpack off her back. She rifled through the contents and pulled out a small container filled with crackers. The kids fell to eating the crackers with a gusto that would have been humorous another time. She yanked out a bottle of water and gave some to one child, then the other, holding it steady even as water dribbled down their chubby chins. Still without a word, she grabbed a second bottle of water from her bag and handed it to Dan. Gratefully, he accepted it and took several thirsty swallows. She took a drink from the one the kids had used before replacing it in the bag.

"Here, let me take that." Dan held out his hand for the backpack.

"But your back," Maggie started to protest.

"It's not really hurt. Mostly my jacket got burned. The fire didn't even touch my clothes. But we don't have time to argue. Got to keep moving."

Her mouth thinned into a determined line, Maggie stood and pulled Siobhan into her arms. Dan hefted Rory onto his hip and led the way in the direction the dispatcher had indicated.

Every now and then, the small group rushed to hide,

crouched down, as a car passed or as noises were heard. Once, they even heard voices nearby. Dan could feel Maggie tremble beside him. He was amazed at how quiet the children were. He kept up a steady litany of prayers under his breath.

"And there it is," he announced almost an hour later. He could see two cars on the side of the road. A man and a woman stood there, apparently exchanging information. Dan recognized them both. When they turned toward him, his trained eyes could make out the shape of concealed weapons under their hoodies.

"Dan," the man greeted him, his voice pitched low. "We have supplies in the trunk. And there are two children's car seats installed, rear-facing, as requested. The tank is full. Do you need further assistance?"

Dan patted the officer on the shoulder. "Thanks, Craig. And you, too, Lori. We will take it from here. But I would appreciate it if you would tail us for a few miles just to be sure we are not being followed."

More police officers.

Maggie had been running for so long, tensing every time she saw someone wearing a badge. Being in such close proximity with so many officers in one day was making her skin itch. They looked decent, though, and Dan clearly trusted them. Although she wasn't ready to trust him implicitly, he had put himself in harm's way several times to keep them safe. That had to say something about the man's character. But she'd been fooled by men before. Her lips twisted as the memory of her stepfather crossed her mind. She shuddered in revulsion. And her real father was no prince, either. Charming on the outside, rotten on the inside. Even her husband had been hiding something. She hurried to stop that thought before she became overwhelmed.

Dan was talking to the officers in a low voice. He seemed at ease. Even so, these new officers were an unknown. She listened intently to their conversation as she loaded up the kids. Her neck felt stiff with tension, and her shoulders were beginning to ache. She fully expected gunmen to erupt from the woods behind them at any moment.

She didn't allow herself to relax her guard until she and Dan were pulling away in the car. The children were holding a babbling conversation in the back, totally unaware of the tense situation. She couldn't remember ever feeling that carefree, that trusting, even as a child. Of course, she'd had the bullies to keep her on her toes then. *I've hidden from someone my whole life.* The revelation did not please her.

"Where are we going?" She gazed out the window as she listened for his response. The trees created a fantastic landscape with their vivid leaves against the blue sky. Dramatic.

"There's a hunting cabin I know of. It's not mine. It belongs to my buddy Jace."

Maggie swiveled her head to rest her gaze on his profile. Strange to notice how handsome he was at a time like this. But he was. His profile was strong. There was something so confident about the way he carried himself. She remembered how quickly he had moved at the house.

Suddenly, he tensed.

"Okay…"

"What? What is it?" Maggie straightened in her seat. "Tell me!"

"It's probably nothing," he stated slowly, though his tone suggested it was very definitely something. "There is a car behind us. I can't be sure, but my gut says we are being followed."

The muscles in her stomach tightened, cramped. She leaned forward slightly, crossing her arms over her stomach in an attempt to hold in the pain. "The other cops—they were behind us," she gasped.

He flashed her a worried glance. "They were. They turned off several miles back. This isn't them."

She peered into the side mirror just as the car sped up, gaining on them.

"Hold on." Dan's mouth tightened into a grim line. His foot pushed down on the gas, and he gripped the steering wheel as he attempted to outmaneuver the other vehicle. Taking one hand off the wheel, he tapped a button on the console area, then replaced his hand on the wheel. *Voice control is a grand thing*, Maggie mused as she listened to him calling the precinct. With as few words as possible he informed the dispatcher of their current situation.

"I'll stay on the line with you until we can intercept you," the dispatcher droned.

Lord, help us. Maggie startled as she realized she was praying. In her experience, prayer really hadn't worked in the past. But as Dan's velocity increased around the curves, she found herself again praying. Now was not the time to reject even the possibility of assistance from God. Hopefully He was still willing to listen to her.

With every twist, the other car followed. Dan's knuckles were white on the steering wheel, but other than that he appeared calm and focused. Maggie aimed another glance at her side mirror and gasped, horror leaping into her chest. A man was leaning out the side window at an impossible angle. The afternoon sunlight flashed against his sunglasses, making it difficult to make out his features clearly. She had no trouble making out the rifle in his hands.

The rifle aimed at their car.

Dan swerved suddenly, just as a shot rang out. It missed the car, but who knew if the second bullet would miss?

"We are one mile from exit 270." He probably didn't realize he was shouting.

"Take the next exit, Lieutenant," the dispatcher directed.

Dan nodded. "On my way off now."

With a quick spin of the wheel, he sent the car hurtling across the lane beside him toward the exit. It was a good thing there was no traffic to speak of. The car following them braked hard to avoid a collision. The man leaning out the window was forced to grab on to the door. She sighed in relief as he dropped the rifle on the road. It bounced and shattered as the rear wheels rolled over it.

As they roared onto the exit, two police cruisers shot into place along the berm, lights flashing. Dan steered off, but the car following them gunned the engine and shot past the exit. One of the police cars sped up the exit ramp the wrong way in pursuit.

Maggie slumped in her seat, drained and exhausted. She stayed in the car as Dan got out to confer with the officers in the remaining cruiser. She lacked the energy even to try to listen to what they were saying. She'd had it. She closed her eyes, not even opening them when the driver's door opened. Dan had returned. She'd known him only a short time, but she already knew the scent of his cologne.

"I checked for bugs. There are no tracking devices on the car. Do you have a cell phone?"

"No."

"Let me check out the diaper bag and the car seats." Fifteen minutes later, she sighed in relief when he announced all clear.

"And do we have another plan?"

"Same plan, Maggie." His voice rumbled. "We are going to continue to the cabin, but via a different route."

Different? The route was an impossible and ridiculous one, Maggie thought hours later. Long drives were one thing, but spending the drive coupled with two children who'd had enough of being strapped into car seats was another. They had allowed themselves the luxury of stopping once for food and diaper changes.

Maggie stepped inside the cabin, Rory sleeping peacefully in her arms. In the past four hours, Dan had made so many turns, she wasn't even positive they were still in Pennsylvania. Not a single landmark was familiar. A bone-chilling weariness settled around her. She was one step away from sliding down that rabbit hole. Between sleep deprivation and stress, she was starting to get a little wacky.

Dan entered, carrying a whiny Siobhan, as she was setting Rory down on a makeshift bed of throw blankets. Maggie wiped her mouth with her hand to cover the smile that was threatening to escape. The poor man was a bit wild around the eyes. His hair was no longer smooth. In places it actually seemed to be standing on end. But Siobhan had taken a liking to him. She whimpered whenever he tried to hand her off to her mother. If Maggie took her, the whimper morphed into a full bellow. She'd offered Dan earplugs at one point, only half joking.

"Do you think I can put her down?" Dan whispered. "I really need to check the perimeter and call my chief. Give him an update."

Maggie stretched out her arms. "Here. Give her to me."

He started to hand her over, then hesitated as Siobhan let out a warning whimper. Maggie took her, anyway. And the bellowing began.

Dan's brow creased. "Are you sure—" he began.

"Go! She'll settle down in a minute." Maggie pointed an imperious finger toward the door.

Dan started to walk toward the door, then stopped with a chuckle. "I can't believe this. You're already telling me what to do."

He disappeared out the door, leaving Maggie standing there, her mouth hanging wide-open. She stared at the door for a couple of seconds before realizing that she was getting nothing accomplished. Shaking herself out of the strange stillness that had come over her, she got her daughter settled with Rory and went to work making the tiny cabin comfortable. She turned on the heat. Hopefully, the place wouldn't take long to warm up, since it was so small.

It was strange. As she waited for Dan to return, she felt uneasy. His presence was so big, so sturdy, that she had felt safe when he was there. Now, knowing that it was only she and the twins, she felt herself tensing as the silence stretched and grew. The wind blew against the little cabin, making creaks and cracks and groans. She felt as if someone was watching her.

A sharp rap sounded on the door. Maggie shrieked. She blushed as the door opened and Dan poked his head around it, his face breaking into a smile. His gray eyes danced.

"Now, who did you think was going to knock before trying to get in the door?" His tone was cocky but his expression was watchful.

"You just startled me, that's all." She chided herself for being so jumpy. Still, the memory of that man coming at her with a knife was looming large in the back of her mind.

The heat clicked on with a loud hum. Dan smiled. "I'm glad you turned the heat on. Not to complain, but it's chilly in here."

"I'm surprised at you. Coming from LaMar Pond, this weather is mild. The winters there are absolutely brutal. But you know that," Maggie responded.

"Well, I'm not actually from LaMar Pond. I'm from Hershey, Pennsylvania. I moved to Pittsburgh when I got out of the army. I moved to LaMar Pond about two years ago. I was working undercover on a case. Actually, I was working to find out what was happening to the jurors from Melanie's trial. Once the case was over, I decided to stay. It's a nice little community. A little slower pace, but I like it."

"Well, anyway, I know it's going to get cold tonight. I figured why wait to warm the place up. I've got warm clothes for the babies, but nothing for me other than what I'm wearing."

"It was a good thought," Dan remarked. "But you won't be staying here tonight."

What? Why stop in such a remote place, why go through the trouble of searching the perimeter if this was only a break?

"Why didn't you tell me that earlier? I thought the plan was for us to stay here. I really don't think the twins can stand being cooped in a car anymore." She looked over to where the twins were settled on the floor. Frustration built as she realized she'd prefer to do just about anything than lug them both back to the car. She was so tired. All she wanted to do was go to bed, although she wasn't sure if she would sleep tonight. Not after what she'd been through that day.

Unease slithered across to her spine and settled in the pit of her stomach. Dan wasn't telling her something. She could tell just by the way he hesitated. He had a look on his face that suggested he was expecting some kind of trouble. Trouble from her.

"Actually, Maggie, you don't need to worry about them riding in a car. You and I aren't staying, but the twins are." She stared at him. He continued, "I called my chief. He has someone coming to meet us here and take protective custody of the children."

"Are you nuts? I'm supposed to leave my children here?" Maggie clenched her teeth to keep from shrieking. The muscles in her throat ached. What was this crazy man thinking?

Dan sighed and ran an impatient hand through his hair. "Look, Maggie, I know this isn't easy to understand. But that scum back at your house was right. Whoever is after you is not going to stop. And you stand out. Even if you shaved your head, you'd stick out. Because how many young women are walking around with twins?"

She opened her mouth to argue.

"Maggie, if this were a normal case, I'd agree you should stay here in protective custody along with the kids. But no one else knows anything about your husband. And no one else can identify the man who killed him. If he is a cop, we have to know immediately. And if he's not, maybe you can help us identify him."

It made sense. Still, she hesitated.

"He's never going to let me be, is he?" she whispered finally. "I don't want to hide, but I'm so afraid for the twins."

Dan rubbed his hand across his neck. She had the sinking feeling he knew something he wasn't telling her. "What?"

"I didn't want to tell you this, but you deserve to know. That gunshot didn't kill Phillip. He was tortured. I doubt he was killed inside the house."

Nausea swirled in her stomach. Poor Phillip. Could she have saved him if she'd tried to help instead of running away?

"Why did I leave him?"

"No, Maggie. No. If you had stayed, you would have died, too. I'm telling you so you understand. This is someone wholly without conscience. In order to protect your children, you have to help us."

He was right. She knew it. Oh, but it was a bitter pill to swallow. She couldn't give in yet.

"What plan do you have to keep them safe?" she whispered. "Dan, these kids are my life. And you are asking me to walk away and leave them with some stranger? Some cop, when you know exactly why I don't trust the police?"

"Not a cop—or at least, not only a cop. And not

exactly a stranger," he hedged. A knock on the door interrupted them. He blew out a relieved breath and went to answer the door. Maggie fumed, arms crossed over her chest. She realized she was grinding her teeth again when her jaw started to ache.

Dan pulled open the door, and Maggie got the shock of her life when a familiar figure stepped across the threshold.

In an instant, she was across the room and wrapped up tight in a vanilla-scented embrace.

"Mom," she choked. Tears streamed down her cheeks, but she didn't care. The frustrations of the past melted as she sobbed like a little girl in her mama's arms.

FIVE

Dan stood, mesmerized, as the two women embraced, rocking back and forth. Tears ran down both their faces. They stood there, laughing and crying, for what seemed like forever. Every now and then one of them would pull back, stare into the other's face, then they would begin the ritual all over again. He felt his throat tighten.

When was the last time anyone had hugged him that hard? Had anyone? Searching his memory, he couldn't remember a single time in his life when he had been the recipient of such an embrace. Surely none of his foster parents had ever touched him with that much affection. He had more memories of slaps and anger than of hugs. He had vague memories of his mother, but she had been gone for so long, they were more impressions than actual memories.

Oh, sure, he had seen people embrace before. His buddy Jace and his new wife, Melanie, were huggers. Not in an obnoxious way. They were just open about their affection for one another. They had the kind of love he'd always wanted for himself.

Stop. Right. Now.

Yes, he was alone, but that was by choice. He never

could explain to any woman what he had become, what he had done over in Afghanistan. He had returned from the war a hero, but part of him had died. It was hard enough for him to pick up his service revolver each morning. He forced himself to do so because he truly believed in the call to serve and protect. But he dreaded the idea that he might actually ever need to use his weapon. That was one reason he had requested the transfer to LaMar Pond. He'd hoped that a small town would have fewer chances for violence.

And now he was looking for a murderer.

What had he gotten himself into?

Dan pulled himself back to the present and saw that the two women had separated and were talking quietly. Anna looked around the room and gasped.

"Are those my grandchildren?" she breathed. Tears once more filled her blue eyes that were so like Maggie's. It was a wonder she had any tears left to cry.

Maggie took her mother's hand and led her over to where the exhausted kids were lying. Neither was asleep. They were both playing quietly with the toys that Maggie had pulled out of her backpack. Anna placed a tender hand on each dark-haired head. Her face was filled with wonder.

"What are their names?" she whispered, not taking her eyes off the two children. The little girl continued playing, but Rory looked up and gave the woman a wide smile. One tooth was just barely starting to poke out of the bottom gums.

"Their names are Rory Sean and Siobhan Anne." Maggie's eyes stayed glued to Anna's face, a hint of worry in their depths.

"Oh!" Anna clapped a hand over her mouth as a single tear ran down her cheek.

"Mom!" Maggie moved forward, her eyes wide with alarm. Her mother just shook her head. When she uncovered her mouth, Dan was astonished to find a huge smile spreading across her face. Maggie blinked.

"It's truly glad I am that you named your children after me and your grandparents. It tells me you've forgiven me."

Maggie bent her head and stared at the floor, her hands shoved into her pockets. After a moment she peeked up, her face sad.

"You didn't need my forgiveness, Mom," she mumbled. "You deserved my respect and understanding. And I was a foolish girl. I'm sorry."

"Margaret Mary, you were a child. I was supposed to have protected you. And I failed both times."

Hmm. Dan was pretty sure one of those times involved Maggie's birth father. Quite a few people were shocked to realize that Senator Joe Travis had several illegitimate children. One was Sylvie, the college student Melanie Swanson had been falsely accused of killing. And another was Maggie. A young Joe Travis had convinced Anna O'Connor to marry him while he was traveling in Ireland twenty-eight years before. Unfortunately, he had neglected to tell his young bride that he already had a wife back in the United States. The whole story had exploded eighteen months ago. Documents found on Maggie's computer had shown that she had discovered the link after the trial and was trying to locate the other children.

"Mom, you did what you could."

"But if you're not angry with me, then why stay away?

Why not let me know where you were, that you were safe? That I was a grandmother? Do you not know the agony I have been through these past two years? First you wouldn't talk to me, then you just up and disappeared. And your lovely house—destroyed!" There was no accusation in Anna Slade's tone, but Dan thought he detected hurt in her voice. Although, maybe it was just the way the Irish accent rounded out the sounds.

Maggie looked at Dan. "Does she know?"

Dan shrugged. How did he know? He hadn't been the one to call her. Knowing Paul as he did, she probably knew only what was absolutely necessary. Paul would have stepped very carefully. He always did.

Maggie placed a trembling hand on her mother's arm. "Mom, I witnessed the murder of my husband. I have been on the run for eighteen months. I was going to call you when the twins were born, but I thought I had been found, so I took off again. I was afraid if I contacted you, you would be in danger, too."

The cop in Dan zeroed in on one thing. Someone had located her a year ago. He needed to get her alone so she could explain that to him. First things first.

"Mrs. Slade, did Chief Kennedy send an officer with you?"

Anna turned her attention to Dan. "Yes, Officer…"

"Lieutenant Willis, ma'am."

Anna nodded her thanks. "Chief Kennedy sent two fine officers with me. Sergeant Thompson and Officer Olsen."

His brows shot upward. Catching himself, he struggled to hide his surprise. Officer Olsen had been a sergeant at one time. Over a year ago, however, he had abandoned his oath as a police officer to terrorize a former convict. Melanie Swanson, now Melanie Tucker, had been convicted of manslaughter. No one knew at the time, but the college girl she had been accused of killing was Miles Olsen's stepsister. He had turned vigilante to attempt to get Melanie to leave town because his stepmother had been grief-stricken over her release. Since he had only tried to scare her and not hurt her, he had received a six-month suspension from the force. Paul was all for a full dismissal, but his boss had overridden him. Still, he'd been on desk duty since he had returned. It was ironic that Paul had allowed him to resume active duty on this case, protecting one of the jurors who had put Melanie in jail.

He went to the cabin door and opened it to peer outside. The two officers were standing there, apparently just waiting.

"You guys planning on coming in?" he called, allowing sarcasm to seep into his voice.

Thompson grinned and bounded up the stairs. He punched Dan in the shoulder on his way past. "Just giving the ladies time, sir."

Olsen stood awkwardly for a moment, shifting his weight back and forth. Finally, he ducked his head, avoiding Dan's eyes, and started forward. Dan stopped him on the porch, waited until the young man met his gaze.

"Officer Olsen, it is against my better judgment to leave you here with that woman and those kids. I don't have a choice, though. But hear me. And understand. You mess up, you let any harm come to them, and I will do my best to see that you never work in law enforcement again. Are we clear?"

Olsen swallowed. He bobbed his head in a nervous nod. "Yes, sir."

There was nothing else he could say. Dan pivoted and followed the younger man back into the cabin. He took a small detour to go into the bathroom and use Jace's first-aid kit to tend to his wounds. Wrapping a bandage around his knee and tending his side took just a few minutes. Leaving the bathroom, he went over to the kids and knelt down, searching one round-cheeked face and then the other. He was actually going to miss these kiddos. Who'd've thought?

Rory was peaceful, as usual. Siobhan seemed to sense that something was off. Her lower lip started to tremble and her big eyes puddled. Panicked, Dan held out his hands.

"Oh, no. Don't cry now, kid. Your mama won't be happy with me if I make you cry."

It was no use. She crawled over to him and pulled herself up on his leg, wobbling as she looked into his face, a tear on each cheek. Dan groaned. He gave in and picked her up. She snuggled in against his shoulder. He felt rather than saw Maggie approach. She smiled at him and her daughter, but her eyes were sad. She probably had never been away from them, he realized.

"Come on, Maggie." He laid a gentle hand on her shoulder and could feel the muscles bunch up beneath his touch. She was so tense it was a wonder she didn't break. He was humbled by her strength. "The sooner we take care of this mess, the sooner you can reclaim your life."

Tears gathered in her eyes. She sniffed and took first her daughter, then her son, into her arms. Dan's throat tightened as he watched her bury her face in her babies' hair and kiss them gently. Then she rose and embraced her mother one final time. Tears swam in her eyes, but she allowed none to escape. He rubbed his chest, trying to ease the constricted feeling.

Finally, she pulled back from Anna's hug. Grasping her arm gently, Dan led her toward the door. He waited for her to exit the cabin, then followed her out. Thompson and Olsen exited the cabin, closing the door behind them. A wail reached through the cabin door, followed closely by a second. The twins, crying for their mother. Maggie's spine went ramrod straight. A ragged sob escaped her throat. Dan reached out a hand to comfort her, but she jerked away from him and ran down the steps to the car.

Give her a moment to compose herself. Swiveling toward Thompson and Olsen, Dan gave the men his hardest military stare. "No mistakes, gentlemen."

When he was certain they understood him, he pivoted on his heel and strode toward the car. He needed to find answers. Then he could return Maggie to her family. Unease pooled in his gut. He felt as though a web was slowly tightening around him. Looking at the woman sitting in the front seat, he strengthened his resolve. There was no room in his life for a woman or kids. Better get this case finished. Why did he feel it was already too late?

Every mile brought her closer to the place she feared most. LaMar Pond. A small blip on the map of rural northwestern Pennsylvania. People were friendly. The scenery was gorgeous—hills and trees and sparkling creeks, or cricks as they were called in these parts.

And someone there wanted her dead.

Would prayer help? She had prayed before, and they had escaped for the moment. Could have been coincidence. Still, if God was willing to overlook her anger and defiance… Nothing made you more willing to rethink your priorities than being shot at and almost being blown up. Her mouth twisted, and she huffed out a soft snort.

"What?"

"Huh?" Angling her head, she squinted at Dan. He had been so quiet as she mused she almost had forgotten she had company.

"You snorted. I was wondering if it was an angry snort or an amused snort."

"I did not snort!"

Dan chuckled. "Yeah, you did. I know a snort when I hear one."

She snorted again in disdain, then slapped a hand over her mouth as he shouted with laughter.

"You gonna tell me *that* wasn't a snort?"

"Fine. I snorted." She rolled her eyes. "I was just thinking of my current situation. It's the kind of scenario I'd expect to see on TV, not in my life. But I guess these past eighteen months should have prepared me for it, to some extent. I think… Oh, I am so not ready for this, Dan!"

While she had been daydreaming, Dan had driven straight to the police station. Her gut roiled, and she seriously thought she might become ill. The image of a man dressed as a police officer holding a gun to Phillip's head flashed through her mind. She was drowning, sinking amid her own memories and fears. She gripped Dan's sleeve, trying to hold herself afloat.

"Hey, Mags. It's okay. I promise." Dan briefly covered her cold hand with his own, warming it. Then he pulled his away, and she shivered, cold again. Her eyes flickered to his face. What was he thinking?

"But what if he's here?" she blurted. "What if I come face-to-face with—"

"Then we'll know." Dan turned off the engine and hesitated. "One thing I want you to tell me before we go inside. You said you thought he'd found you a year ago?"

Maggie sucked in her breath. The man never missed anything. She blew out a hard breath. He needed to know. "Just before the twins were born. I was living in a shelter. One day, I saw a couple of guys come in. Something about them seemed off. I hid, and I saw them passing my picture around. I didn't wait to find out what they wanted. I took off. I remembered Wendy from college and took a chance. It was a good one. She's the one who got me into a clinic for homeless and indigent people where I had the twins under an assumed name. Then she offered me her house while she was gone. She had been planning on finding someone anyway, so it had worked out. She even let me buy the cribs and other baby stuff under her name."

"Huh. I'd wondered how you had the kids off the radar." He opened the door and stepped out of the car, his movements stiff and jerky. His leg. And his side. How had she forgotten his injuries? His determination to aid her, to defend her, helped her decide. She would be strong. After all, he was right. If she wanted any sort of life, she needed to know who had killed her husband and why. She needed to put this whole thing behind her. She remembered only too well what it felt like to be a target. That was not a legacy she wanted to pass on to Rory and Siobhan. Her breath hitched in her throat at the thought of her babies, but she forced herself to keep moving.

Although she made sure she was always within arm's reach of Dan. He was the one with the gun, she reasoned.

Far too soon, she was settled in a chair inside Chief Paul Kennedy's office, Dan standing beside her as he reported to his chief. Maggie allowed herself to examine him. A handsome man with close-cropped dark hair and gentle brown eyes, he exuded calm and authority. But he was an unknown to her. Automatically she shifted her focus to Dan. Despite his tattered appearance, she instinctively felt safe as long as he was near. And that scared her. Her twins needed her. She couldn't allow herself to depend too heavily on another person, especially a man.

She brought herself back to the conversation when she heard the chief addressing her.

"Ms. Slade, I can't tell you how relieved we are that you have been found safe and sound. I aim to keep you that way. We are a small department, so we don't have an official sketch artist. One of the officers from a neighboring department helps us out. She'll be available tomorrow afternoon. In the meantime, we need you to look at some pictures of our officers to see if any of them are familiar to you."

She swallowed. Her mouth was bone-dry, and her legs shook. Somehow, she managed to walk over to a table where the photos of all the officers had been placed. Setting her jaw, she scrutinized each picture.

One face looked familiar. Reaching out, she tapped the picture with her finger. "It wasn't him, but he looks very familiar to me."

"That's Lieutenant Jace Tucker," Dan replied, leaning over her shoulder. Her shoulder tingled where he brushed against it. "He testified at Melanie's trial as the arresting officer. They're married now."

"She married the cop who arrested her? Amazing."

Dan just grinned. Maggie went back to perusing the pictures. After she had gone through the officers without any success, Paul had her go through the photos in the criminal database. Nothing there, either. Her heart was leaden in her chest.

"So we're no closer," she mourned.

"Not true, Maggie," Dan countered swiftly. "We now know that whoever killed your husband was not a cop."

"And we know something else," Chief Kennedy broke in. "I checked out the information that Ms. Slade gave you, Dan. The same day she was married, that chapel in Las Vegas was broken into. The files containing the weddings that happened that month were destroyed."

Maggie's heart sped up. She placed a hand over it, feeling it pound.

"That can't be a coincidence." She lifted her eyes to Dan, then turned them on Chief Kennedy. "Can it?"

The chief was already shaking his head. Dan was tapping a fist absently against the desktop, his gaze narrow.

"No, it's not a coincidence. Dan?"

"I agree, Chief. Someone had something to hide. Only question is, was it someone after your husband, or was it something your husband planned?"

What?

"Phillip? I can't imagine Phillip being involved with something like that."

No. It just wasn't possible. Okay, so he obviously hadn't been completely honest with her, but Phillip had been a very gentle man, totally opposed to violence of any kind. It was unthinkable that he would be involved in anything like this.

"Fortunately," Chief Kennedy's drawl broke into her chaotic thoughts, "the perp was caught. A man named Robert Hutchins. He insisted that he had acted alone. He was also found guilty of tampering with documents at the courthouse where he worked. Specifically, applications for wedding licenses from that week."

"So that's why we never found any evidence of your marriage," Dan mused, his eyes thoughtful. "It's possible that the person or people after your husband didn't even know about you until they entered your house. My guess is that as soon as they saw the wedding pictures, you became a target. Even if you hadn't gone home right then, you would have still been in danger."

The chief nodded in agreement. "Tomorrow, you can start checking out these leads. It's too late for you to do anything more tonight." He rose from his seat. "Oh, by the way, the Pittsburgh precinct called. Chief Garraway is on medical leave for the next couple of weeks—her arm was broken in two places. She also had a couple of ribs broken. But they were clean breaks, so the doctors expect a full recovery."

Dan blew out his breath in a whoosh, his face lighter than it had been five minutes before.

"So what do we do now?" Dan's voice was soft. Maggie could hear the exhaustion in his tone. He was practically asleep on his feet.

"You two need to get yourselves checked out. Get

a good night's sleep, then you can head out in the morning."

"My other house—"

"I'm sorry, Ms. Slade." Chief Kennedy's eyes were sympathetic. "Your house went through foreclosure last spring."

Maggie deflated.

"Most of your possessions were put into storage. And the house you were renovating with your husband was destroyed by arson. I believe you already know about that."

Had she ever felt more defeated? Maggie had weathered some tough storms in her life, but this was the worst. Where was she supposed to go? Now that she was here in LaMar Pond, she was exposed. The feeling of safety she had felt beside Dan earlier had fled. She had never been so alone in her life.

A hand on her shoulder startled her. She jerked her head up and locked eyes with Dan. His face had an odd expression. His eyes were sympathetic, but the tension in his face clearly showed he was deliberately keeping himself distant from her. She could almost imagine an invisible barrier between them. Obviously, the man had issues. But it was sweet that he was concerned.

She turned her attention to the matter at hand.

"So if I can't go home, where should I go tonight?"

Dan nodded, as if he approved of her pragmatic approach.

Chief Kennedy rubbed his chin. "Well, now. I'm not comfortable with the idea of you staying in a hotel. It would be too hard to secure. It's too late to call anyone else, although I'm sure Jace and Mel would let you stay at their house."

"Mel? You mean Melanie, the woman I helped to put in jail?" Oh, now *that* would be comfortable.

"I told you she doesn't hold a grudge." Dan's soft admonishment reached her ears.

"Maybe not, but I am not going to encroach on her. I can't imagine a more awkward setup."

She twisted her neck just in time to see Dan roll his eyes and catch his muttered word. "Women." Maggie decided to ignore him.

Chief Kennedy appeared to come to a decision. "It's not ideal, but I propose that you bunk down here. We have a break room for the officers. It has a couch. You can grab a few hours of sleep in there."

Panicked, her eyes flew to Dan. He tilted his head and regarded the chief. "I'm not leaving her here alone, Paul. I'll bunk down in the room across the hall. No one uses that room this time of night anyhow. But I can't be on guard. I'm too beat to be of any use. Who else is on the schedule?"

"Jackson is on call. He went out to handle a domestic dispute but should be back before too long. Want me to hang out until he gets back?"

"Nah," Dan said, yawning. "We'll be fine. You go on home."

Chief Kennedy made sure she was as comfortable as she could be in a police station. She smiled a little at the irony of her situation, although she wasn't feeling that amused. Across the hall, she could hear Dan moving around as he set up a cot.

I hope he's not in pain.

A sound outside her door broke into her thoughts. She stuck her head out to see what was going on. And gasped to see that Dan had set himself up in a folding chair outside her door. She bit her lip, her throat aching as tenderness welled inside her. His face was white and drawn, and she could see him struggling to remain awake. Yet here he was, again putting her safety above his own needs. It was one of the most selfless things she had ever witnessed. But she didn't want to have him on her conscience.

"Dan," she whispered. "You should lie down and go to sleep. I'll be fine."

"Maggie," he growled back. "Shut up. Go to bed. I'm only here until Jackson gets in."

She should be offended that he'd talked to her that way. She really should. But it was difficult to work up any real indignation between the exhaustion and the amusement.

She lay down on the cot and pulled the blankets that Chief Kennedy had provided over herself. Snuggling down, she drifted into a dreamless sleep.

And jolted awake when a rough hand was put across her mouth.

SIX

Her heart slammed against her chest and her breath caught in her throat. A whimper escaped, muffled by the masculine hand covering her mouth. Fully awake now, she started to struggle, working to free her arms from the blanket.

"Oof!" her assailant muttered as her elbow found his stomach.

"Maggie, it's me!" Dan hissed against her ear.

"Dan! What—"

The hand was replaced over her mouth. "Hush. Something's wrong. The lights went out, and someone's here."

"Jackson?"

He was close enough for her to feel his head shake. His lips touched her ear as he whispered as low as possible. "He called. He had to go to a car crash. No one else has any legitimate reason to be here at this hour. *Shh!*"

There. She heard it. Slow, deliberate footsteps. Whoever was here was doing their best to be silent. But their shoes creaked. Otherwise, they would have had no warning. Through the open door that led out into the hall, Maggie saw a beam of light sweep past. She stiffened. It looked as though whoever was out there had gone into the room where Dan was supposed to be sleeping. That meant her room was next.

A tug at her hand had her moving instinctively. She didn't question Dan as he led her through a connecting door and out into another hallway. He had to be itching to go after whoever was in the other room, but she had learned enough about him to know that he would get her out of the way first.

A single beam of light erupted in front of them. Dan was using the flashlight app on his phone. A crash sounded in the distance. Their stalker evidently had discovered they were missing and knew his cover had been blown. He had given up stealth and was now searching with a vengeance.

Heart pounding in her ears, Maggie pressed closer to Dan as he led her to a door and opened it with irritating slowness. Every nerve ending in her body screamed, *Hurry!* She jammed a fist in her mouth to keep from involuntarily whimpering. Even as she trembled with urgency, she understood. If they made a sound, their stalker would find them. Although Maggie wasn't real confident that they'd be able to elude him for long. How big was the LaMar Pond police station, anyway?

Finally, Dan nudged her toward the half-open door.

"Careful." His breath fanned her neck as he whispered tensely in her ear.

They were going to the basement. Dan brushed past her, no doubt to protect her in case she missed her footing. Gripping the railing with both hands, Maggie prayed she wouldn't fall even as Dan's phone flashed a dim path in front of her. Praying? That made twice in less than two days. That was some kind of record for her, since she hadn't prayed since that awful day...

She closed her mind to the past and refocused her attention on the steps ahead of her. Near the bottom, she did indeed slip. A gasp escaped her lips as her ankle twisted and her body lurched forward. Her fall was stopped as Dan caught her. She was aware of the muscular arms tightening around her briefly before he set her back on the floor.

In the darkness, he grabbed her hand and pulled her forward. She did her best to walk without complaining despite the pain shooting up her left leg with every step. In her mind, she remembered the way Dan had kept going, even after being stabbed and having his jacket catch on fire. Surely she could handle a twisted ankle without complaint. Hopefully, he wouldn't notice. She knew how protective he was.

They moved through the room and out into what seemed like the longest corridor ever. Every now and then, the flashlight would land on a window. At one point she distinctly saw the words *Caution: Shooting Range*. She shivered. *We're walking targets right now.*

"Can you walk a little farther, or is your ankle really hurting?" Dan's husky whisper made her grimace. So much for him not noticing.

A door banged open before she had a chance to answer. The basement lights flared to life. Footsteps thudded down the steps. *Out of time.* Dan shoved Maggie into the first door on the left, followed her inside and shut the door behind them. A click told her he had locked the door. She doubted that would keep anyone out for long. But it gave them a few more seconds. Maybe even minutes.

Dan flipped on the light. It was pointless to work in the dark when whoever was behind them knew they were here. Maggie followed him to the far wall. There was a window near the ceiling. Despair trickled down her throat. It was only a window well, not a full window. Would they fit? Sure, she was small, but Dan... She cast her eyes at his wide, muscular shoulders, then back at the window, biting her lip. There was no way he would fit through.

Pacing the area, his face a fierce mask of concentration, Dan searched for a way out. He grabbed a pipe and swung, grunting as it connected with the window. Glass shattered. Two more swings and the window was cleared. He shrugged out of his jacket and tossed it over the jagged edges of glass still in the windowsill. He turned and motioned Maggie forward.

"But, Dan, you won't fit," she protested.

"Don't worry about me." He urged her forward, dragging a table under the window. Without pause, he placed his warm hands around her waist and lifted her onto the table. "You need to go. I sent a text to Paul and Jace as soon as I realized what was happening. For all I know, they may already be here—there's no signal down here. Take my cell and hit number two as soon as you're in range. That's Paul's cell."

She touched his shoulder gently, nodded her understanding. She slipped his cell into her back pocket. She could do this; he was depending on her. Pressing her lips together, she faced the window. With his hands giving her a boost, she dragged and pulled herself through.

She was halfway through when the doorknob rattled. She doubled her efforts, ignoring the pain as a piece of glass sliced into her right arm. Grunting, she forced herself through the narrow space. A gunshot. The stalker had shot the door. Probably to get rid of the lock. She'd almost made it when the door burst open. Just as she pulled through, the brick next to her legs pinged. The bullet had literally missed her by an inch. A second shot followed.

"No!" Dan's voice, raised in a harsh shout.

Crack!

Silence.

Urgency made her hands shake as she grabbed Dan's phone and dialed.

"Dan, we're here. I heard shots."

Maggie cut off the chief. She'd worry about her manners later.

"In the basement. Dan made me go out through a window. He's still inside. I think he might have been shot." Her voice was thick with tears. She hadn't even realized she was crying.

"Get away from that window!" Maggie swung around as the cop she'd recognized earlier rounded the corner at a full-out run. Lieutenant Tucker. Dan's friend. He reached her and dragged her away from danger. "How many shots?"

Focus, Maggie. Dan needs you. Dan.

"Four. The first shot through the lock. One hit the window just before I escaped. The other two..." She choked off, unable to continue. What if Dan was dead? It would be her fault.

Dan was frozen. Numb. His hands continued to shake, even after he dropped the gun. He couldn't tear his eyes away from the man lying on the floor. Dead. Because he had shot him.

The man had been aiming for Maggie, he reminded himself. The first shot had hit the wall inches from where Maggie had been pulling herself through the window. Then he had shifted, fired at Dan, forcing him to dive behind a filing cabinet for cover. Then he had lined up a third shot. Aimed at Maggie. Dan knew he'd never reach the man in time to grab him before he could fire. He had had no choice. He'd pulled out his gun and shot. The first time he'd shot at anyone since his disastrous second tour in Afghanistan. It was a clear-cut case of self-defense.

But someone was dead, and he was to blame.

Again.

Even worse, he knew the man. Not very well, granted. Dennis had been a competent dispatcher for the police department, but he had been surly on his good days. Still, Dan never would have pegged him for a killer. Yet, here he was. Dead.

Dead, dead, dead.

A tortured groan escaped. Images flooded his mind. Shells falling. Faces surrounded him, silently begging him to save them as the shelter burned around them. A young woman, hair on fire—

No! He was more than that one moment in time. He couldn't let himself dwell on it. It would drown him, pull him under if he let it. Maggie. Oh, no, where was Maggie? Had she gotten hold of Paul? Pointedly ignoring the prone body on the dirty floor, he strode toward the door. He needed to make sure Maggie was alive and well. He quickened his pace, ignoring twinges in his side. Pain was irrelevant. All that mattered was making sure another citizen didn't die on his watch. Not ever again. An image of Rory and Siobhan came to mind.

He couldn't let any more kids become orphans because of his failure.

He was met in the hall by Jace. His friend grabbed his arm. He winced. He had slammed against the brick wall to get behind the filing cabinet. He had escaped being shot, but barely.

"Dude! Are you okay? We heard shots. Maggie's in hysterics. She thinks you were killed."

"She's okay? I was afraid a stray bullet might have hit her."

Jace placed a comforting hand on his shoulder. "She's fine. Shook-up. She's very worried about you, though. Paul is making her stay in his office, getting a statement, that kind of thing. He can't let her come down and interfere with a crime scene. But it's about killing him to stay up there. He's pretty shook-up, too. Hold on." Jace used the radio clipped to his shoulder to let Paul know he had found Dan, to all appearances safe. Dan could hear Maggie talking in the background.

He needed to sit. Hearing Maggie's voice, knowing she was safe, had the strangest effect on him. He started shaking, and his balance was off.

"Dan? Buddy, you are white as a ghost. Did I miss something—are you hurt?" The warmth and concern in Jace's voice was a new thing. So was his pleasure at hearing it. Dan liked his isolated life. Instead of friends, he was used to having only acquaintances. He had not confessed his fears to a soul. Yet, here was Jace, acting the part of a good friend despite Dan's reticence.

And he was glad.

Because right now, he could use a friend.

Jace was talking.

"...and the perp? What is his condition?"

Dan swallowed around a tongue suddenly too large for his mouth. He couldn't tell if he was going to vomit. Fortunately, he was disciplined enough to keep his reactions and emotions under wraps. He focused all his attention on the details. The details always helped him to distance himself.

"He's dead. I shot him after he got off two shots and was going for a third. He was aiming for the window when I fired."

Maggie's legs, still visible as Dennis started to pull the trigger...

He gave his head one hard shake to clear it. "We're gonna have to call Chuck to come get the body before we can get a team in there to process the scene." He wasn't going to be happy. The coroner was a man of integrity and honor. He was also a bear before 8:00 a.m. and three cups of coffee. He was downright scary in the middle of the night.

"He's gonna be real happy," Jace groaned, echoing Dan's thoughts, his hand going to his radio to call in the necessary personnel.

"Jace." Dan halted him before he could activate their response team. "Dude, it was Dennis. Dennis Purchard."

"Dennis! The dispatcher?" Jace jerked his head toward the room Dan had vacated. He started to speak, shook his head, then looked Dan in the eye. "I know he wasn't a very pleasant fella, but man, I never thought he was the kind to gun down someone in cold blood."

"Me, neither." A thought struck him. "When did he start working here?"

Scratching his head, Jace scowled thoughtfully. "You know, I'm not sure. It's been at least seven or eight years. We'll check. But after this scene is processed and you give your statement."

As expected, Chuck arrived stomping and growling. His growling stopped, though, when he spotted the body. The sight of any young man dead by violence was always a shock. Add to that the fact that everyone who worked in law enforcement in the county had known and trusted Dennis.

Wordlessly, Chuck motioned to his assistant. The young woman stepped forward, hands trembling as she took out a digital camera and photographed the scene. Dan and Jace stood inside the doorway making sure no one entered or left the scene. At one point, a young officer started to unwrap a piece of gum, no doubt because of nerves. Dan barked out a harsh reprimand. Proper procedure demanded no eating or drinking while processing a crime scene. In his book, that included gum chewing. All they needed was for some young kid to contaminate the scene by accidently dropping the wrapper or spitting out his gum.

When Chuck was satisfied that his assistant had done a thorough job, he had the body hoisted onto a stretcher. Dan couldn't stand it anymore. He bolted for the stairs, taking them two at a time. He burst through the door at the top of the stairs and headed straight for Chief Kennedy's office. After poking his head in, he took in the scene. The tightness in his chest eased when he noticed Maggie sitting on the desk while a paramedic tended a cut on her arm. He frowned. It looked pretty deep. She'd probably got caught on the glass as she'd slid through the window. It had ripped her shirt from shoulder to elbow. But she had escaped.

A hint of blue ink on her right shoulder snagged his attention.

"You have a tattoo?" he blurted.

"Dan! Are you okay?" Maggie made a move as if to jump off the table.

"Hey, don't move!" The paramedic's sharp voice stopped her. Dan recognized her but couldn't recall her name. Cindy? Susan?

A grimace crossed Maggie's face. "Sorry."

Feeling more in control now that he had found her, Dan sauntered into the room and leaned his uninjured shoulder against the filing cabinet. He made note of the fact that the cut on her arm seemed to be her only injury.

"I never figured you for a tattoo girl. What is it?"

The paramedic finished and backed away. Maggie murmured her thanks in a distracted tone, her eyes still on Dan. She grabbed a flapping bit of the ripped fabric and eased it back, revealing an intricate tattoo. The blue was the sky surrounding a butterfly. There were letters around the wings of the butterfly, but they weren't in English.

"Uh, Maggie? What does it say?" He squinted, tilting his head so he could see it better.

"It says *Is maith an scáthán súil charad.*" The foreign words flowed smoothly from her mouth, the cadence definitely Gaelic. The corners of her lips were tucked in. He was willing to bet she was biting back a grin.

"Yeah, I kinda figured. In English?"

"It means 'A friend's eye is a good mirror.'" She hesitated. "I got it when I was sixteen."

"Your mom let you get a tattoo?"

There was that grin again, although it was a little

strained. "Well, she didn't exactly know about it. I got it in a fit of rebellion. And to honor my grandmother."

"Is that something your grandmother used to say?"

"Not really, but it's an Irish proverb. She made me a quilt once with a bunch of proverbs embroidered on it." She smirked. "My favorite is *Ná glac pioc comhairle gan comhairle ban*, which means 'Never take advice without a woman's guidance.'"

Dan laughed, shaking his head.

The paramedic packed up her bag. Maggie slid off the desk and walked over to Dan. Voices in the hallway signaled that the coroner was leaving. Dan heard Paul's voice. He went to the door and looked out. Paul and Chuck were standing together in the hallway. Paul's face was white and drawn, his normal, cheerful demeanor dimmed by the night's events.

"Chuck, is it true? Dennis was our shooter?"

"I'm afraid so, Paul. Here, see for yourself." Chuck gently uncovered Dennis's face so Paul could see. Dan saw a white face, then looked away. A sharp gasp had his head swiveling in the opposite direction.

Maggie was standing in the doorway next to him. The blood had leeched from her face, and her hand was covering her mouth. She swayed, and Dan reached out, afraid she would faint.

"Maggie, you don't need to see this," Dan started, concerned.

She didn't appear to hear him.

"That's him. That's the man who shot Phillip."

SEVEN

Maggie held the coffee cup between her hands. She wasn't normally a coffee drinker, but at the moment she welcomed the heat seeping into her chilled palms. Each sip of the bitter coffee seemed to calm her jangled nerves just a little more. She closed her eyes briefly but popped them open again a second later. She couldn't get his face out of her mind. And even though he was dead, she could hear his voice as if she had just heard it, instead of a year and a half ago.

"Ms. Slade, are you sure the man chasing you was the same man who killed your husband?" Chief Kennedy sat across from her, his gaze serious. She felt bad. He looked like a man who'd had a really rough night.

Maggie nodded. "Yes, sir. I have seen that face in my nightmares for a long time now."

"It explains one thing, Chief."

Dan pulled a folding chair over and swung it around so he could straddle it, his arms resting on the back. If she weren't so tired, she might have smiled. It was so typically male.

"Yes, Dan? What does it explain?"

"The man Maggie saw shoot her husband was dressed

in a LaMar Pond PD uniform. Purchard could easily have snagged a uniform from a locker and returned it before it was noticed." He narrowed his eyes. Maggie could almost hear his mind racing. "It also explains how Maggie was found. He had access to a lot of intel. It was no secret that I had gone to Pittsburgh several times on leads. I suspected yesterday that my car might have a tracking device on it. Or maybe it was a bug. Can't prove it, since it's a pile of ash. But I'm pretty convinced."

Chief Kennedy pursed his lips, stirring his own coffee as he deliberated. Finally, he nodded. "Yeah, I can see that. Ms. Slade, what did he say to your husband?"

She did not want to have to do this again, but what choice did she have?

"He said Phillip had something and needed to give it back. To his boss," she added, remembering suddenly. "He never identified who the boss was. Or what exactly Phillip supposedly had."

"What do you think he might have stolen?" The chief's question was casual, but Maggie heard the underlying question. *And were you involved, too?*

Her spine stiffened in outrage. Jutting out her jaw, she glared at the chief. Then she turned her furious gaze on Dan for good measure. "I don't think he stole anything, *sir*." She was too angry to care how rude she sounded. She had been hounded, separated from her babies, shot at, attacked and finally awoken in the dead of night to flee another attack. And now these men sat here practically accusing *her* of wrongdoing. Well, no more. She had had enough.

"Sir," Dan cut in, "I think we need to follow our original plan. The man who is in jail for breaking and entering the chapel might have known something. I think Maggie and I should go there and talk to him."

There was a knock on the door before Chief Kennedy could answer. Lieutenant Tucker. He looked exhausted, but determined. As he passed behind them, she noticed he clapped a supportive hand on Dan's shoulder. He handed a file and a camera to Chief Kennedy. Briefly, she wondered if she should excuse herself so they could conference. But they would ask her to leave if they needed to, wouldn't they?

"Lieutenant Tucker," Chief Kennedy said with a stern glare, "we have a civilian present."

"Understood, Chief. But I would suggest we don't want to let her on her own just yet."

A fierce scowl on his face, Chief Kennedy leveled a flat stare on her. She sat straighter and tried her best not to glare back. She wanted him on her side, but she hated feeling as if she were being judged. All she wanted was her life back. And to get that, she needed this man's assistance.

After a few tense moments, Chief Kennedy nodded, although clearly not convinced.

"I'll agree that Ms. Slade needs to be kept in the loop, and because someone is obviously after her, she needs to be protected."

She released her breath. It was going to work out.

"How deep do you think Dennis was, sir?" Dan shifted a stress ball from one hand to the other. Maggie doubted he even knew what he was doing. His brows were drawn together as he considered the situation.

"I don't think Dennis was a key player. He's been working here for eight years. The information I found on Phillip Nelson indicates that he was only in the area for about five."

Her mind reeled at the way these people casually spoke about Phillip. They were focused on the job at hand. She understood that.

"Maggie, we don't mean to be insensitive," Dan murmured.

She startled. Her hurt must have shown on her face.

"He's right, Ms. Slade," Chief Kennedy agreed. "But we have to be objective if we are to find who is after you and help you get back to your normal life."

Okay, she was definitely on board with that.

"All righty, then." Chief Kennedy rubbed his hands together, then reached for the phone. "You two need to visit the prison in Vegas, while Jace and I—"

Maggie interrupted him. "Sir, before we get too far ahead, when will I be able to contact my mother? I need to check on my children."

Silence met her question. Realizing she was drumming her fingers against her thigh, she forced herself to relax. At least on the outside. Inside, her stomach muscles cramped, and her heart was thudding. *Oh, please. I just need to know how my babies are doing.* A light hand brushed her shoulder. Then it was gone. Dan.

"Mags, I wish you could contact her—for your peace of mind, if nothing else."

"But why can't I—"

"Shh." She glared at him. Arrogant man, telling her to shush. But the gentle expression in his eyes melted some of her anger. *He truly cares*, she marveled. "They are with two officers and their grandmother. We have no idea who is orchestrating any of this. Until we do, they are safer if we don't contact them. You know I'm right, don't you?"

"Argh!" she yelled. The three men stared at her, wide-eyed. "Aye, I know you are right. But I'm not likin' it at all, and that's a fact." She crossed her arms over her chest and slumped in her seat. Part of her was embarrassed to be acting so childishly. But mostly she was so frustrated she felt she could blow at any second.

A chuckle to her left caught her off guard. Shifting on her chair, she glared at Dan, incensed that he seemed to find her situation amusing.

Raising his hands to halt her fury, he shook his head and got himself back under control.

"I'm sorry, Maggie. I'm not laughing at your situation. Honestly, I'm not. I'm a little punchy right now."

She continued to stare him down, unimpressed.

He shrugged. "Your accent gets really strong when you're emotional. Did you know that?"

Blinking, she gawked at him. "Aye, so I have heard."

She blew out a quick breath, sending her bangs flying upward. There was a dull ache inside her chest. She had never been so far from her children. They were her life. The entire reason she had been able to keep going for so long. She hated being separated from them, but she knew that until this impossible situation was resolved, she couldn't return to them. At least she knew that if something happened to her, her mother would take care of them. Sorrow crept into her heart. She had blamed her mother for so long. But now she understood that her mother had had no control over what had happened to her. If Anna had known what would happen to Maggie, she would have sacrificed anything to stop it. Having kids of her own helped Maggie finally understand and forgive. But she had wasted so much time. She hoped with all her heart she would have the chance to make amends for her stubbornness.

Maggie's mobile face twisted with one volatile emotion after another. Dan wished he could give her what she wanted. He couldn't imagine what she was suffering, being apart from her kids, not knowing for sure what was happening. But he knew they needed to move, keep ahead of whoever wanted her dead.

"How 'bout we get some plane tickets to Vegas?"

The next hour was a blur. Paul dealt with the aftermath of the shooting spree in the basement. Somehow, the bloodhounds, meaning the press, had caught wind of something going down at the police station. The three major news stations had trucks and camera crews set up right outside. The newspapers had photographers and journalists on hand, as well. Paul was at his urbane best, deflecting questions that were too close, answering those he could with dignity and charm. He would not give out the name of the shooter or the officer who had taken him down.

An hour later they were on a flight from Erie to Pittsburgh, where they would catch a second plane to Vegas. They were fortunate. The layover time was relatively short. Actually, it was nonexistent. They had to walk as fast as they could to board the second plane before the doors closed. They were in relatively secluded seats.

Maggie sighed. "I wonder if we're being followed now."

"Paul bought us a little time," Dan murmured to Maggie. He kept his voice low, just in case. She raised a brow in question. "Whoever is calling the shots here will probably guess that Dennis was the shooter. That can't be helped. Although the guy behind all this seems to have a lot of people willing to kill for him, I am really praying he is running out of resources. After all, he's lost the man who attacked you in your house, the men in the car who blew up the gas station and now Dennis."

"Is that just a figure of speech?"

"Huh? What do you mean?" Dan's heart lurched as he peered into Maggie's shadowed face. It was more than strain from the recent events. He could almost feel a struggle going on inside her.

She slumped back in her seat, a bleak look on her face. She turned her head toward him, her mouth trembling. He was struck by the memory of a young girl he had known briefly in Afghanistan. He had never even asked her name. But her large eyes, so empty and bewildered, had haunted him these past three years. Except Maggie's eyes weren't empty, he reminded himself. She still had her children to go back to, to give her something to live for. He would do all he could to see that she returned to them. And then he would walk away. He had to. He steeled himself against any foolish dreams that wanted to take root and focused on his mission.

"Is what a figure of speech?" he asked her, more to distract himself from his musings than anything else.

"You said you were praying the man who wants to kill me runs out of resources," she explained. "Are you really praying about that, even when you are in danger?"

"Especially when I'm in danger."

She looked lost and he struggled for the right words. How do you explain faith?

"I'm not going to lie and say that I have always prayed. I was a foster kid in Pittsburgh. By the time

I was fifteen I'd been in four different homes, two of which were abusive. I had a chip on my shoulder the size of Texas, and I couldn't seem to stay out of trouble. When I was about sixteen, I had my first run-in with the law. I ended up in Chief Garraway's office. She looked right at me and told me straight-out I could either plan on a life of crime, which would end with me in jail, or I could get my head on straight and make something of my life. I don't know how to explain how much she impressed me. She believed in me. And she was the first person I'd ever known who was a Christian, and she inspired me to find my own faith. Well, it wasn't easy, but I got myself straightened out, and I joined the military. That's when I decided to be a cop. I was fortunate to be able to find a job in Chief Garraway's department."

"I thought you served two tours of duty." Her voice was soft, unsure.

He closed his eyes briefly and bowed his head. "Yeah. My unit got called back. I can tell you the faith I developed because of Chief Garraway was the only thing that kept me sane while I was in Afghanistan. I got sent home after I was injured on a mission." Dan pressed his lips together tightly. He wanted her to understand. He wanted her to know that faith was a good thing. But there were things from his past he just wasn't ready to share yet. And maybe he never would be.

Maggie lifted her head off her seat and leaned forward, her eyes filled with compassion. She raised one trembling hand and laid it on his cheek. It was a gesture of affection, but even more than that it was a gesture of one who recognized suffering all too well.

"I used to have faith," she whispered. Dan leaned forward just a little bit in order to hear her better.

"Growing up my family never had much. You know I was born in Ireland?"

Dan held his breath, feeling he was on the brink of discovering what made her tick. He was filled with the sense that what he said or did in the next few moments would impact Maggie's faith, or lack thereof, for the rest of her life. It's a very frightening feeling to know you could affect somebody's soul that much.

"My mom and I, we lived with my grandmother. When I was about, oh, I don't know, five or six, we were able to move to the States. I never really understood how we had the money to do that. We had always been poor. And when we arrived in the States, we were still poor. My mom worked two jobs, but she always had time for me."

Maggie's eyes grew distant, clouded over with the force of her memories. Her accent grew stronger, letting him know better than words that her emotions were running high. "Even though we were poor, we were happy. I remember going to church every week with my grandmother, and she would pray with me whenever my mother wasn't home. She died when I was ten. I was so desperately sad. But I knew, I just knew that I would see her again in heaven. I never doubted that. Until my mom married."

A chill traveled up Dan's spine. Some instinct warned him that he wasn't going to like what he heard next. He also knew that this was not a story Maggie told to many people. His fingers curled into fists as he waited.

"At first, I was happy she married. Some of the kids at school had started to pick on me, bully me. I talked different. I wore the same clothes again and again because we couldn't afford more. My stepfather was a really nice guy. And I used to confide in him. Until I was twelve. My mom had taken a new job and she worked third shift. Then he started getting really creepy, following me around, making comments about how pretty and grown-up I was. It freaked me out. I started to avoid him, but he was always there. I even woke up one night to find him sitting beside my bed, just watching me." She shuddered. Her head bent forward and her hair swung to hide her face like a dark curtain. He saw the way her shoulders hunched, and anger started to burn in his gut. She was ashamed, even though she was the one who had been taken advantage of. She had been a child and had done nothing wrong.

"Mags, you don't have to—" Dan started to interrupt her. She shook her head.

"I need to get this out of my system, Dan. It's poison. And you are the only person I trust enough to tell."

A tremor shook him. She trusted him. *Him.*

"I don't know what would have happened. He was killed in a car accident two weeks later. It devastated my mom. But I was so relieved. I had been so scared, and then he was gone."

"Maggie, did you ever tell your mom?"

She rocked in her seat, her arms tight around her stomach. She shook her head, but a low sob erupted from her mouth. He wanted to touch her, to comfort her, but was afraid to cause her to recoil. Who knew how fragile she was right now?

"I didn't need to. My mom found pictures. He had been taking pictures of me when I thought I was alone. Sharing them with his friends."

His throat burned as bile hit it. He swallowed, keeping himself still with an effort. "One of his friends must have left the pictures out. Because two months later, a boy at school was passing them around."

He couldn't take it anymore. With an exclamation, he reached over and hauled her trembling form into his arms, rocking her as he would a child. She resisted at first, her body stiff. Then she slumped against him. A drop splashed on his hand. With care, he wiped her tears off her cheeks.

"I had to leave school. Parents started calling, complaining that their children had to be exposed to someone like me," she continued, her voice thick, hitching every few words. "We changed our phone number because we were getting crank calls. I was homeschooled until high school. By then we lived in a different district, and no one knew me. But I was always scared someone would point me out. I kept to myself. And I didn't pray anymore. How could God have let that happen?"

Before he could respond, the flight attendant came on the intercom. The plane was starting its descent. Maggie pulled away to sit all the way against the back of her seat, her hands gripping her armrests. Dan saw her gulp. Poor Mags. She hadn't admitted she was terrified of flying. But it was written in every line of her body. He took her hand in his and gripped it. Then grunted. She probably didn't even realize how hard she was squeezing his hand. Well, if it made her feel better, he would let her—even though he wouldn't be surprised if she left a bruise.

He couldn't leave her last question completely unanswered, though. He leaned close to her ear.

"Maggie?"

"What?" He nearly smiled at her strangled tone.

"God did step in. He took your stepfather out of the equation before he could physically harm you, and He gave you a mother who took action to protect you in every way she could."

"Maybe. But there was one thing she never did, and I held it against her for years because I didn't understand."

Dan frowned. "What else could she have done, Mags?"

She was prevented from answering when the captain's voice echoed over the intercom, thanking them for flying with them. In minutes, they were disembarking, merging with the other passengers. Dan's senses went on high alert. As unlikely as it was, every cell in his body was attuned to any sign they were being followed. He hurried Maggie along, anxious to get her out of the open.

He was unable to relax until they were tucked inside a taxi, putting distance between themselves and the airport.

Could he bring up the topic of Maggie's stepfather again? It didn't seem like a good idea. Maggie probably wouldn't want to discuss him in the back of the cab.

"Did you know my father is Senator Travis?"

Startled, he blinked at her.

"Um, yeah. It came up while we were trying to find out who was after Melanie."

She gave a brisk nod. "He gave my mom money for her silence about their sham of a marriage. Enough to help us come to the States. So she wouldn't talk—to the press or to anyone. She never even told me he was my father. I had to find out on my own. Can you imagine?"

"When did you put it all together?"

"I found out about the senator around the time of the

trial while looking through some files my mom had asked me to help her organize. About a year and a half after the trial ended, I found out that I had several half sisters. I was shocked to realize that Sylvie had been one of them."

"I can't even imagine how you felt," he said gently.

She grimaced. "At the time, I was furious. Not only about the secrets, but also because I felt he got off easy while we were struggling."

The taxi pulled up to the prison. Dan stepped out and paid the driver. They watched the taxi pull away. He turned back to Maggie.

"He might seem to have gotten off easy, Mags, but in the end he's the one who lost out. He missed getting to know you. And he probably has no idea he's a grandfather. Gotta feel sorry for a man like that. After all, who can say they've really lived when they haven't had their hair pulled by Siobhan?"

He was hoping to make her smile, but instead she laughed out loud. Her eyes, which had seemed so empty and despairing moments before, filled once more with humor and light.

Maggie might be struggling to believe in God, but as far as Dan was concerned, that laugh and the warmth it brought back to her face was nothing short of an answered prayer.

EIGHT

Dan leaned back in his chair, looking around the room with a casualness he was far from feeling. The only sound in the room was the steady tapping of Maggie's feet on the bare floor as they waited for the inmate to be brought in.

Nothing about this room was comfortable. The chairs were hard and bolted to the floor. The walls were barren, except for warnings plastered against them. Tilting his head up, Dan read, "Please keep hands in plain sight at all times." Office-like cubicles with phones broke up the long row of the counter, while the bulletproof glass added an extra touch of menace.

The door opened and a middle-aged man stepped through. Robert Hutchins. His shoulders were stooped slightly, and his faded brown hair was thinning on top. His hands were cuffed together. His face fell when he caught sight of Maggie, and a hopelessness entered his expression. This didn't look like a hardened criminal, but rather like a man beaten down by life.

He shuffled over to a stool on his side of the glass and sat, reaching for a phone. Both Maggie and Dan copied his movement so they could converse.

"Malcolm's dead, isn't he?" The question shot out of the man across from them. Dan raised his eyebrows. Maggie's mouth fell open. She pulled the phone away from her ear and frowned at it. As she replaced it against her ear, she narrowed her eyes at him.

"I'm sorry, Malcolm? I don't know any Malcolm."

Robert sneered, contempt in his eyes. "No, you wouldn't have. You knew him as Phillip."

Dan had suspected that Phillip was not Maggie's late husband's real name. "I take it you were closely acquainted with him?"

But how closely? Was this man also involved with those hunting Maggie down?

"Yeah, you could say that." Robert looked at them, his lips twisting. "His real name was Malcolm Phillip Hutchins. He was my brother."

A shocked silence followed this announcement. Robert chuckled. It was not a pleasant sound. The glance he leveled at Maggie was filled with derision. In fact, he looked at her almost as if he hated her. Had he ever met her?

"I don't understand," Maggie burst out. "Why would he give me a false name? Why wouldn't Phillip, I mean Malcolm, tell me who he really was? I wasn't a stranger! I was his wife."

"You were his *current* wife," Robert taunted her. He seemed to take pleasure in adding to her pain. "He was married before, when he was still going by the name Malcolm."

Dan had put up with all the cruelty he was going to take from this guy. Who did he think he was to talk to Maggie this way? She was an innocent in all this. He no longer doubted that Maggie knew nothing about what her late husband had been involved with. But this guy, brother or not, had been in it deep enough that he had broken into the wedding chapel, destroyed legal documents. Dan just had to find out why.

"Enough with the attitude. I need you to start from the beginning. Whoever killed your brother is still out there, and he is still willing to kill. I need to know why."

Even though the light was dim, Dan could still see the way that Robert paled. A look of terror entered his eyes. His hand on the phone started to shake.

"I can't be seen talking to you!" Robert dropped the phone and jumped to his feet. He backed toward the door. The prison guard stopped him without saying a word. It was obvious that Robert was not going back to his cell until Dan said they were done. He said something to the impassive guard, but all Dan could make out was the desperation in his tone. When the guard merely pointed to the phone he had dropped, Robert snatched it up. "Don't you see what's going to happen?" he shrieked. "If anyone finds out that I was talking to you, if anyone knows that I had a clue about what happened to Malcolm, I could be in danger, too."

Maggie and Dan both held the phones away from their ears, wincing.

"Okay, calm down and stop shouting," Dan ordered the older man.

Robert meant every word he said. His fear was nearly tangible. But Dan had to focus on the danger to Maggie, Siobhan and Rory. Just thinking about the twins strengthened his resolve. He would solve this and make Maggie safe so she could be with her children. And continue to make amends with her mom.

"Just tell me what you know. As soon as we know what's happening, we'll leave you alone."

Nervously, Robert lowered himself down onto the stool again. His contemptuous expression had vanished, leaving a much shaken man in its place. Beads of sweat dotted his forehead.

"Okay, let's try this again," Dan said. "I need to understand what happened. Let's go back to the beginning. Why was your brother using a fake name?" Dan kept his voice as soothing as possible. He held the phone in his left hand, his right hand he kept below the counter so that Robert couldn't see it, and reached out to grip Maggie's fingers. He could feel her shaking. He squeezed, just to let her know she was not alone. Then he dropped her hand.

Robert leaned his elbows on the counter and covered his eyes with the hand holding the phone. "It started about, oh, about six years ago. My brother and his wife Lily were having trouble. Money troubles. Lily worked as a nurse, and my brother worked at a tool and die company in Cleveland. They had school loans they were still paying back. So Malcolm decided to take a second job. And at first the job seemed to be good for them. He was working at a family business. It was a men's clothing warehouse, and he really liked it." Robert wiped his sweaty forehead on the sleeve of his prison shirt, leaving a wet spot.

"Lily began to notice strange things, though. Malcolm was agitated. He was working strange hours and was acting secretive. She tried to talk to him, but he would just get angry. She told me she thought he was having an affair. He denied it, but when she told him she wanted him to quit that second job, he said he couldn't do it. She ended up leaving him. About six months later, Malcolm called me in the middle of the night. It turned out that his new boss was running a money laundering business. Malcolm was working in the finance department. He had found some evidence early on, back when he was still with Lily, but was making good money, so he kept his mouth shut. When the boss realized he wasn't planning on talking, Malcolm was given more work—and more pay to stay quiet about it. Then some feds showed up one day at his house. I'm not sure of the whole story, but he agreed to get evidence for them if they would give him protection and clear him of any charges for what he had done. Well, he gave them evidence, and his boss sent some goons to kill him. The feds decided they couldn't protect him unless he went into the Witness Protection Program. So he became Phillip."

Maggie sat forward, her face intense. Her eyes blazed into Robert's. A hot, angry flush stained her cheeks.

"Correct me if I'm wrong, but I thought that in the Witness Protection Program you cut all ties with your former life. How is it that you were still in touch with your brother?"

It was a fair question. One that Dan had planned to ask himself.

"He did cut ties with me," Robert protested. "At least for the first six months. But we had always been really close, and he didn't have anybody else to talk to. He called me one day and told me what had happened. He also told me that he had kept some evidence from the feds. He wanted to have some kind of leverage just in case his old boss ever came after him."

Dan and Maggie both sat up straight. They looked at

each other and then at him. Dan felt a tingle of excitement. This could be huge. All he needed was one break, and he could find the man behind all this. "What evidence did he keep?" He couldn't quite keep the urgency from his tone.

But Robert just shook his head helplessly. "I have no idea. Maybe some pictures, maybe he taped something. I don't know. I told him he should let me know, but he just said I would be in danger if I knew."

"Tell me about the break-in."

"I hadn't heard from Malcolm in a while. He called me out of the blue one day and said he'd fallen in love again. He planned to marry this girl, but she didn't know anything about him. He needed my help. My brother was afraid that the people who were after him might have found out his new identity. He was paranoid that way. So when he wanted to get married, he called me 'cause he knew I would help him make sure her name wouldn't be officially tied to his. I was working at the courthouse, so I was able to go into the computer after hours and delete the application you'd filed that day. He called me later and begged me to make sure the certificate wasn't filed. He couldn't let the marriage information make it into public record, where there might be some kind of automatic search for his name. So I agreed to take care of it."

"But you got caught!" Maggie blurted. "And now you are in jail for helping your brother."

"Well, I never told anyone why I broke into the wedding chapel. Once the files were destroyed, the evidence of his marriage was gone."

Dan was honestly curious. "Why not just tell people

why you had resorted to a criminal act? It might have made the jury more sympathetic."

Robert gave him a pitying look. "He was my kid brother. If anyone knew I had done that to help him, who knows what could have happened. Anyway, I got five years. At the time I thought it was worth it to protect him."

"I get the feeling you helped your brother out of lots of messes through the years," Dan mused. He stopped himself from using the word *enabling*, but it wasn't easy.

"Your brother died a year and a half ago," Maggie said gently. "The federal agents knew about it. Didn't they let you know?"

A weary sigh escaped him. His chin sank down onto his chest. "Yeah, they told me. But I was hoping that it meant that they were just relocating him with a different alias. You know what I mean?"

Dan nodded. Something else had occurred to him. "When we entered, you looked at her." He pointed to Maggie. "It was almost like you knew her."

"I never saw her before, no, but Malcolm had sent me a picture." Meeting Maggie's eyes, he shook his head. "Meeting you killed him, you know."

Maggie didn't think anything else could shock her, but those words combined with the venom in Robert's tone sent her reeling. She reared back in her seat, gasping.

"Excuse me?"

"Hey," Dan protested. "That's—"

Robert made an angry motion with his hand. His face hardened. "He had to fall in love with someone working for the press!"

"But I wasn't working as a reporter," Maggie protested, pressing her free hand tight against her abdomen. "I was an entry-level fact-checker It never even occurred to me that my husband was leading a double life."

The man on the other side of the glass flushed. A vein pulsed at his temple. "He wasn't living a double life! He had left everything behind to start over with a new life. And because of your job, he lost even that!"

A gentle hand touched her wrist. Maggie turned her gaze to Dan. He gave no outward indication that he had touched her. His body was leaning forward, his eyes focused on Robert. But his hand below the counter brushed her wrist again. She understood. He needed her to calm down and let him take the lead. It was the only way to get the information they needed.

It went against the grain, but she leaned back in her chair and allowed Dan to take the lead. Part of her wanted to flee so she would not learn about her husband's past. How could she ever take anyone at face value again? The man she had loved, the only man she had let that close since her stepfather's betrayal, had been lying to her all along. She hadn't known him at all. It felt like a new betrayal.

Setting her jaw, she steeled herself for whatever else she might learn. Flicking a glance at Dan, she saw that even with his longer hair, he looked 100 percent cop. It was in the level stare he settled on Robert. A stare that said he would brook no lies.

"I need to know everything, and I need to know it now. People's lives are in danger as we sit here."

My babies. The thought flashed across Maggie's mind, reminding her how important it was for her to focus.

Robert swallowed. "I don't know everything. I know that Malcolm had a zip drive on him with information against his old boss. He took her—" he jerked a thumb in Maggie's direction "—out for dinner and realized the drive was gone. The next morning, he stopped by her office and found it lying under a pile of papers on her desk. He took it home and hid it. But two days later, the information he had on the drive appeared in a column in the *Journal*. Nothing that accused anyone of anything, but just enough to arouse suspicion."

Maggie shot forward in her seat. "I never saw any zip drive! And I had nothing to do with writing articles."

"Maybe not, but obviously someone else took the opportunity to swipe it during the night."

Guilt swamped her. She pushed it aside. There was no way she could accept responsibility for that. If the information was that sensitive, Phillip, or Malcolm, should have kept it locked away from the start.

"What information?" Dan ground out, probably clenching his teeth. Yep, that jaw was tight. "Which columnist?"

"I don't know. All I know is that he tried to keep an eye on the man in question for a few days. And he was convinced he was sniffing around for more information. He was positive he was correct when the man was killed four days later."

"Brandon Steel!" Maggie gasped. "I remember now! The police thought he had died during a random mugging."

She shuddered, remembering walking past his empty desk. She had never liked Brandon. He had been a player and a dishonest one at that. It had also been rumored that he came by his information illegally. But he wrote well, and his cutting wit sold papers. The people in charge were willing to overlook his lack of ethics as long as he brought readers to the newsstands, and as long as he never got caught doing anything illegal.

It had never crossed her mind that he had gotten information from foraging stuff from his coworkers' desks. It didn't surprise her, though.

She was so lost in her own thoughts that she started when Dan touched her elbow. Jerking up her head, she saw with astonishment that Robert was being led through the door back to his cell. Dan was standing next to her seat, concern shadowing his warm gray eyes.

"Maggie? You okay?" His deep voice sent a shiver down her spine.

She cleared her throat. Straightening her shoulders, she stood, careful not to stand too close to him. The man was starting to mess with her senses.

"Fine. Just thinking."

Fortunately, Dan didn't press her for more details. Instead, he gave a slight nod. His hand was warm on the small of her back as he wordlessly guided her toward the exit. Funny how it both comforted and unsettled her.

A kaleidoscope of thoughts whirled in her head, making her feel light-headed. The effort to hold a conversation was beyond her capabilities at the moment. Dan appeared to be likewise preoccupied, his brows lowered and a wrinkle carved into his forehead.

They caught a taxi back to the airport. Maggie leaned her head against the window and closed her eyes. It was the only way she could be alone with her thoughts. Sort them out so they could make sense. Inches away from her, she could hear the clicking sound of Dan's fingers on his phone as he tapped out a detailed email report to Chief Kennedy. It would be so easy, she thought, to reach out and grab his hand. Just to assure herself of… what?

In reaction to her irrational thought, she flexed the fingers of the hand lying on the seat between them. Suddenly, she was filled with the urge to ask him his impressions of the interview with Robert. Biting her lip, she stared out the window, biding her time.

The remainder of the drive to the airport was completed in silence. No longer a comfortable silence, though. Maggie had gotten used to Dan, she realized. Used to him enough that she didn't feel the need to fill the space between them with banal conversation. But now, when she wanted to talk, she felt the presence of the taxi driver. Tension filled the cab like a thick, oily fog, making her feel as if she couldn't get a full breath.

It was with great relief that she stumbled out of the cab outside the airport. Drawing the air deep into her lungs, she waited for Dan to pay the cab driver, then followed when Dan took off at a brisk stride toward their gate. The urgency in his pace was contagious. She was getting paranoid, she thought, constantly feeling as if someone was watching them. She forced herself to move faster. He looked back at her, consternation filling his expression as he shortened his strides to match hers.

"You should have told me I was going too fast," he reprimanded her.

Heat crawled into her already-warm cheeks. "I didn't want to slow us down." *Or appear weak.*

A snort from her companion let her know he wasn't impressed. "Next time say something. I wouldn't want to leave you behind by accident."

The fear of being watched continued until they were

seated on the plane. She sank into her window seat with a sigh. Her arm was jostled as Dan situated himself beside her. Their arms touched as he diligently scanned the other passengers. It would have been easy enough to casually readjust her posture so that their arms weren't touching. She knew it would. But she didn't. Nor did she allow herself the luxury of examining why beyond that she felt safe.

The com system dinged as the flight attendant's voice filled the cabin. At the direction to put all cellular devices on airplane mode, Dan scowled. So Mr. Confident didn't like being disconnected. Interesting.

Maggie attempted some light conversation, just enough to keep her mind occupied. For her efforts, she got one-word answers and several eye rolls. Clearly, someone was not feeling communicative.

She huffed back in her seat, feeling childish, but also so jumpy she positively itched with it. She tapped her fingernails on the plastic armrest, getting some satisfaction out of the staccato sound. A large hand covered hers, stopping the motion.

She slanted her eyes toward Dan and saw a smile hovering around his mouth. Well, glad she could amuse him!

"Maggie, it's going to be a long enough flight. Please settle down." His deep voice was barely above a whisper, but she heard it just fine.

"I can't," she hissed back. "I miss my kids, my husband was a liar, someone's after us and, on top of that, I'm terrified of flying!" The last word left her mouth, resulting in chuckles around them. She blushed as she realized her voice had risen with her last complaint. "Sorry," she whispered, mortified.

The hand on hers tightened. "I noticed you seemed frightened on the airplane out. But you handled it well."

"I was acting on autopilot."

"Maggie, I need some quiet to process everything we've learned. I am not ignoring you, but I need to think. I will keep you safe."

Guilt swamped her. This man had suffered injuries for her, and she was whining like a two-year-old because he wouldn't play Distract Maggie. She ducked her head and absently traced the fingers of her free hand over the back of his. There were several scars, she noted idly. This was a man who wasn't afraid to put himself in danger for others. His muscles tensed as she gently rubbed the scars. Burn scars, if she wasn't mistaken.

"I'm sorry. I'll let you think. I don't mean to be a pain."

She started to pull her hand out from under his. In a surprising turn of events, he wouldn't let her. She raised her eyes to meet his, but he was looking away again, lost in thought. So she let the hand lie still beneath his.

Looking for something else to calm and center her thoughts, she was surprised when the idea popped into her head: Why not pray?

Pray? Where had that thought come from? Oh, sure, she had prayed before, but…

She couldn't really think of a good reason not to pray. She certainly had nothing to lose for trying, and she apparently had the time. *Here goes*, she thought.

Okay, God. I hope You're still listening to me. I'm not sure what to say. Please, Lord, my kids need me. Please let me survive. Get me home to them. And please protect Dan. And heal his scars, whatever they are. Uh, thanks. I mean…Amen.

A sense of peace flooded her, making her eyes sting. She marveled at it. Never in her memories could she recall feeling the presence of God, but she felt it now. Soothed and comforted by it, she drifted off to sleep.

A long while later, Maggie awoke when the flight attendant announced they could turn their devices back on. The city below was becoming clearer. Wow. They were already descending. Sometime during the flight Dan had released her hand. Maggie couldn't wait to tell Dan what had happened. He was looking at his phone again, she noticed with a grin. She reached out to him, thinking of getting his attention. All thought of telling him vanished a second later when he broke the silence with a shocked exclamation.

Dread curdled in the pit of her stomach.

NINE

Quickly, she sat up, alert, her eyes wide. Her throat was dry and her heart pounded.

"What's wrong? Is someone hurt? My kids…" A shaking hand went to her throat, her imagination running wild. She barely noticed the slight lurch as the plane touched down.

It was Dan who reached across the seat to her. He took the hand nearest him, gently prying the clenched fingers open so he could hold the hand. His thumb rubbed in soothing circles on her palm.

"Shh, Maggie, Siobhan and Rory are fine. So is your mom."

"Then what is it?"

Shaking his head, he sighed. "I guess you need to know. Wait until we get off the plane, though." Without moving his head, his eyes slid to the side, clearly indicating the other passengers surrounding them.

The tension returned as she waited. And waited. How long did it take to taxi to a gate, anyway? The view outside the window came to a halt as the plane stopped. Finally, people started to move. She jiggled her leg up and down while waiting. As soon as it was their turn to move, she shot out of her seat and into the aisle, only to have to wait again for the passengers in front of her to mosey off the plane.

The second they had cleared the ramp, she grabbed Dan's uninjured arm and dragged him to an empty corner. "Spit it out!" She rounded on him, arms folded across her chest.

"Paul had a phone call from the prison. Robert Hutchins was found—dead. He'd been strangled during work detail not long after we left."

Maggie swayed. His hand flashed out to steady her. She allowed the contact for a few seconds before stepping back.

"What else?" She knew he wasn't done.

"We had to sign in. Whoever ordered the hit would have found out who was visiting and where we're from."

"So we're targets? Again?"

When would it end?

"I don't know. I can't promise we're off the radar." Dan ran a hand over his chin. "What I do know is that there is no way I'm gonna let you step foot on another airplane. The only way we could have gotten here this fast was by plane. There's only one flight from here to Erie for the rest of the day. We'd be trapped and putting others in danger if they're watching for us at the other end."

"Um, how will we get back to LaMar Pond?" She planted one hand on her hip and tilted her head, frowning.

He flashed a weak grin. Oh, no. she wasn't going to like it, whatever it was.

"Relax, Mags. I got it covered."

"Yeah, I can tell. If you're so confident, why don't you just tell me what we're going to do?"

Casting a wary glance around, he pulled her deeper into a corner, backing her in so that her back was to the wall. If anyone came after them, they would have to get through Dan before they could get to her. She suddenly had to swallow past a lump. It was such an automatic move on his part. Instinct, she thought.

"I sent a text to one of my foster brothers," he rumbled. "An alternative mode of transportation is on its way. We just have to wait. And keep vigilant until it arrives."

"An alternative mode of transportation? You mean a car."

Slowly, he shook his head. Not looking good.

"What exactly—"

"Trust me," he murmured.

She did trust him. But she still wanted to know.

"Dan," she began in her most threatening tone.

"I'm starved," he butted in. "Let's see if we can get something to eat, then go somewhere out of the way. Somewhere we can see and not be seen."

And that was as much as she was going to get. She opened her mouth to argue, then stopped. He was rubbing his side again. A sigh escaped as she gave in. *He's probably faking, just so I will feel sorry for him and give in. It's working.* With a scowl, she followed silently.

"How many foster siblings do you have?"

Dan shrugged. "I had several through the years. Ty was the only one I was ever close to. I didn't bother to stay in touch with the others."

His phone whistled. He showed her the text from Chief Kennedy. Someone had been asking about them, her specifically, at the Erie airport that morning.

"Paul had called security at the airports. He was to

be notified of anyone asking about us. That's how they knew where we were headed."

"What about privacy laws?"

"Nothing is absolutely private."

He sent a quick text back to the chief. Within a minute, another call came through.

"Ah." Dan nodded. "The man in question did not buy a ticket."

"So we're good?"

"Not yet. Just because he didn't doesn't mean someone else didn't. If I were them, I would have someone else on the plane. That way airport security wouldn't view the person as suspicious."

"That makes sense." Too much sense.

Minutes later, she had reason to be grateful for Chief Kennedy's warning. With a suddenness that made her stumble, Dan jerked her into a gift store.

"I feel like a human-size yo-yo," she groused.

"Sorry," came his distracted reply.

Following the line of his gaze, she swallowed a gasp. A woman was out there showing her picture to passersby. People were stopping and talking to her. Her face was earnest and desperate. Maggie had a clear image of the photo she was passing around. It was a picture from before she had disappeared. Her face had been fuller then—she had been newly pregnant. And her eyes and lips were made-up.

"Wonder what she's telling them. What an actress."

"We have to hide your hair," Dan whispered.

"Maybe a ball cap?"

He eyed her, lips pursed and brows furrowed before he discarded the idea. "Too much hair. Hold on. Keep low." He marched away. She went to the T-shirt rack and kept her face hidden as best she could. Soon he was back with a hooded sweatshirt. She quickly donned the shirt and pulled up the hood.

"Good. Good. Slouch your shoulders a bit. Yeah, like that. Put your hands in the front pocket. Eyes down. Sweet." He started to head out the door.

"Wait! Are you crazy? She's still there."

"Honey, as long as you keep your eyes down and don't smile, we should be fine." Dan pulled a ball cap out of the plastic gift shop bag he was holding, put it on and left—motioned her to follow. Maggie was relieved to see that he at least had the sense not to approach the woman. He skirted behind her while she was talking with someone else and pulled Maggie into the midst of the crowd heading to the shuttle. They drifted just close enough for them to hear the woman say "…my sister. I need to catch her…father ill…"

Maggie held in a snort with difficulty.

"I'm sending a text to Paul. She needs to be detained, but I can't alert security without endangering you," Dan murmured.

They flowed with the shuttle line, eventually boarding the bus. They got off on the other side of the airport and immediately joined in with another crowd, trying to blend in. Maggie's patience was wearing thin when Dan's phone whistled again.

A wide grin spread across Dan's face. Her breath caught in her throat. He was magnificent. She crushed the thought as soon as she realized what she was thinking. But she couldn't quite stem the tide of color flowing up her neck and into her face. Grateful for the hoodie, she tucked her head inside the hood.

"Good news, Maggie. Our ride is here."

Somehow she didn't think this was going to make her as happy as it did him.

She was right. Dan raised expectant eyebrows. There was only one thing she could say.

"You have got to be kidding me."

Dan refused to let her lack of enthusiasm dampen his. He felt like a kid. It had been years since he had ridden his motorcycle. And what a gorgeous bike it was! All black and shining silver. He had lent it to Ty before going to Afghanistan. Between his combat injuries and his work schedule, he'd never gotten around to getting it back. So Ty had kept it with him in Pittsburgh. Dan ran a hand over the seat. Man, he was happy to have her back.

"Dude, thanks!" He slapped hands together in a shake with Ty. His foster brother hadn't changed a bit. Still fit and muscular, with an engaging air about him. His dark curls and skin hinted at his Mexican-American heritage. He looked like a young man without a care, but Dan knew he had some deep scars. Scars just as deep as Dan's.

"No problem. She has gas. I kept the inspection good, and she's been taken out regularly," Ty answered easily, his attention wandering to Maggie with open curiosity.

"Don't have time to talk, buddy. We are in a police situation. I'll call you later."

"Sure, I understand." Ty's open smile vanished, replaced by concern. "You be careful. If I don't hear from you in a couple days, I will not be happy. *Si?*"

Dan rolled his eyes, but he really didn't mind. Very few people had ever shown concern for his well-being.

He was starting to get used to people caring for him. "*Si*. I will call you."

"Good."

"The helmets are in the truck." Ty sauntered over to his truck and tossed two helmets to Dan, who handed one to Maggie. She held out her hands for it with obvious reluctance, her pert little nose wrinkling. He bit back a smile. She sure was a spunky thing.

Slamming the helmet on his head, Dan swung a leg over and kicked the bike into gear. He couldn't contain his smile. Just for kicks, he revved the engine. He grinned at Maggie and laughed as she gingerly placed the helmet on her head. She stepped up to the bike with great care, as if it were a living animal ready to bite her. Dan motioned for her to climb on. She did so, but it was obvious she had no idea how to sit. He helped her situate herself, then took off. Her shriek nearly deafened him on one side. It didn't matter.

He swerved through traffic, always with care. When possible, he got off the interstate so they could avoid traffic jams. Not to mention, he thought they had a better chance of arriving safely if he kept a low profile. Even though he hadn't been seen on the bike for years, better safe than sorry.

As he took a tight curve, he felt Maggie's arms grip his middle harder. He was conscious of her tucked up against his back. She hadn't wanted to get on the bike, but she hadn't complained, either. She was brave, he thought again. If he'd had the time, he would have taken a more scenic route. Certainly, he wouldn't be traveling with any traffic. But time was one thing they were short on.

On another occasion, he might have enjoyed the ride.

Right at the moment, though, he felt vulnerable. His shoulder blades were tight, and every now and then he felt like twitching. It was as if he was under a microscope. He couldn't help but think they might as well have painted a bull's-eye on their backs.

On Maggie's back.

Man, he hated that she was such an easy target. How could he protect her if someone started shooting from behind? Dan didn't like not having that kind of control. Suddenly, the excitement he had felt when Ty had brought the old bike melted, morphed into a grim determination. He had forgotten his past, his failures, for a small time while enjoying this ride with a beautiful woman whom, he suspected, he was beginning to have stronger feelings for than was safe. What had started as a quest to redeem himself and bring a woman home safe to make up for those he had allowed to die had become personal. He needed to get this done. Fast. But he had a sinking feeling that he was too late to save himself from a broken heart.

It was nightfall before they finally arrived in LaMar Pond. The small town was lit up, and the main street was far more crowded than normal, even for a Saturday evening. Dan parked his motorcycle near the library. The town square was blocked off. There was a local band belting out popular country tunes in the gazebo, which was situated in the center of town. Traffic that normally would flow around the square in one direction was nonexistent, the streets crowded instead with vendors and customers.

Maggie slid off the back of the motorcycle, gripping his arm to steady herself. She kept hanging on as she took in the crowds and lights around her, wide-eyed. She inhaled deeply, closing her eyes. Dan smiled.

"Heritage Days. I had forgotten they do this every fall. I bet they had the parade this afternoon, didn't they?"

"Yeah, I guess. I don't usually go. I'm not a parade person." Dan wasn't prepared for the way she swung around to face him, way too close. But she didn't back away. Maybe she didn't notice that she was in his personal space bubble, but he sure did.

"Not like parades! Are you feeling okay?" She laid a hand on his forehead in mock concern. As her hand touched his face, his skin tingled with awareness. Her startled eyes connected with his. Electricity hummed between them. Heat climbed into her cheeks, and he suspected his own face had gone a shade pinker.

Pulling her hand back as if stung, Maggie stumbled back from him. As she moved away, he breathed easier. She shifted her gaze awkwardly.

"Um, parades," she stammered. "Yeah, I love them. I can't wait to take the twins to one. As soon as this mess is finished, I mean."

She was babbling. So she had felt the attraction, too. And like him, she seemed to want to ignore it. That was fine with him. Peachy, in fact. So why did he feel disappointed?

A blaze of color burst in the sky above them. Fireworks. Great.

A cold sweat broke out on Dan's brow. There was no way he could stay and watch. And he sure didn't want Maggie to witness what was sure to come. He grabbed her hand and began pulling her away from the square.

"Come on," he snapped, urgency making his voice harsh. "We can't stay here. Too open."

Too late.

A white flare burst above them, the resounding boom echoing like a gunshot. *Exactly* like a gunshot. The sound swallowed him. Caught him up in the snare of memories. Gunshots. Fire. Screams. He couldn't save her. His clothes were on fire. But he couldn't get to her. Or get the kid. They were going to die. And it was his fault.

TEN

"Dan? Dan!" Maggie grabbed at his arms. He pushed her back. She grabbed again and bodily dragged him behind a hot sausage vendor and into an alley. No one appeared to pay any mind to them. The crowd was too busy oohing and ahhing over the dazzling fireworks. Any other time she would have been doing the same. But right now all her attention was focused on the man in front of her. Her heart ached at the lost look on his face. That strong face that was now twisted in anguish.

"Can't," he gasped.

"Dan?"

"Can't get her out. My fault. She's gonna die. My fault. Should have gotten here faster. Should have…"

"Dan! Snap out of it! No one's caught! No one's dying." Maggie grabbed on to his jacket and shook him, gently at first, then harder when he didn't react. "Dan! Look at me. Please? It's me, Maggie."

At her name, he looked down at her as if seeing her from a distance. He frowned. Then his eyes widened, horrified.

"Maggie?" His arms reached up to grab on to her

wrists. She hadn't realized she was still gripping his jacket. "What happened? Where are we?"

She was reluctant to answer. Some inner feeling told her he knew exactly what had happened, but he was too ashamed to discuss it.

"The fireworks started and you had some sort of, um, I think it was a flashback?" Her sentence ended on a question. She had never encountered a person caught in a flashback before, although she had read about them. "I dragged you into an alley. I don't think anyone saw us."

His head flopped forward, rested on the top of her head. He heaved a sigh that stirred her bangs. "I was afraid that would happen. Fireworks are one of my triggers."

Leaning back so she could see him, she pulled one wrist from his grasp. He lifted his head slightly but stilled when she ran her free hand down the side of his face. It was a tender gesture, one she used to calm the twins when they were upset. When she realized what she had done, she was shocked and started to withdraw her hand. He caught it again. Keeping her hand in his, he started walking down the alley.

She tugged him to a stop. He avoided her eyes.

"Dan, tell me what happened. Please?"

His mouth tightened. He tilted his face so that his expression was hidden, but she was relentless. Bending, she moved so she was in his line of vision. Oh, the poor man. His pain was almost tangible.

"I don't speak of it. Ever."

"You need to. Honestly, Dan, I understand the macho image thing. But you're a cop…you can't afford for this to happen if you hear a gun shot in the line of duty."

He reared back. She had struck a nerve. Good. It

pained her to hurt him, but he needed to admit that he needed help.

"Fine, but we need to keep moving. Every moment we stand still is a moment more we give the enemy to find us."

She nodded. They started off at a brisk pace. At the intersection, Dan stopped and flattened himself against the building, motioning for Maggie to do the same. He cautiously peered around the corner. Maggie tensed. What if someone was there? Apparently, no one was, because he soon gestured to her and started moving again. Fast. She jogged to keep up.

"That's one of the reasons I moved to LaMar Pond permanently," he murmured, a wry twist to his lips. "I figured the small town would have less excitement. You know, quiet and dull."

The last was said with sarcasm. She smiled. These past few days had been the antithesis of dull. The urge to smile faded as quickly as it had come.

"So this has never happened on the job?"

"When I shot Dennis, I froze up. For just a few minutes. I literally couldn't move. Terrified me. But I knew you were counting on me, so I packed it in. A soldier doesn't leave civilians unprotected."

She knew he had been a soldier. He must have seen terrible things. It explained a lot.

"Before that?"

"I had trouble dealing with loud noises. I'd get jumpy if a car backfired. I can't go to Civil War reenactments anymore. I hate that. I always loved those. Revolutionary War ones, too. But now… War is an ugly business.

"My squad was ordered to evacuate a small village under attack. A house was on fire. I ran in to help get everyone out. I thought I was done when I heard the screams." He shuddered, sweat beading on his forehead. But he forced himself to continue. "A young woman was caught inside with her son. I ran inside to get them. I can still remember the sounds, the roar as the room started to burn. The woman had been injured, and I couldn't carry both her and the child. So I took the boy, and I promised I would come back for her. I don't even know if she understood me. I got him out and handed him to the first person I saw. Then I ran back inside."

He stopped again. A single tear ran down his face. Maggie wanted to wipe it off, to tell him it was okay. But it wasn't.

"I could hear her screaming inside." His voice was raw. "It was a scream of agony. I tried to go to her, but people were holding me back. I managed to break free but only got about two feet inside when the ceiling collapsed."

Wetness dropped onto her hands. She was crying. Using her sleeve, she wiped the tears away. Bracing herself on the wall for a moment, she went to the brave man before her and wrapped her arms around his waist. Her only thought was to comfort him.

"I could feel the fire on my back. I still have scars. But what haunts me is her face. I was sure I saw it before the ceiling collapsed. Maybe it's just my imagination. But it haunts me. And the sound, the one that makes me cringe, is the loud crack the ceiling made right before it crashed down on her. I hope it killed her instantly. I pray that she didn't burn to death."

His phone beeped. Instantly he broke off his story to answer.

"Hey, Paul. What's the news?"

His face darkened. Maggie shivered. Whatever it was, it couldn't have been good.

"Right. Can you pick us up?" He gave their location, then hung up. "Paul says not to go to the station. They found evidence that Dennis has been keeping tabs on me for months. Paul is unsure if his office is a secure location at the moment. So we are going to his house to discuss what's been going on."

Tension she hadn't realized she was feeling drained from her shoulders. The idea of being a sitting duck at the station held no appeal. Just because Dennis was dead didn't mean it was safe. After all, they had been found at the airport, hadn't they? Being in any public location made her skin itch. Other than Dan, any person walking by could be a threat.

They settled down to wait for Paul to arrive. Part of her wanted to ask what had happened to the boy, the one Dan had saved. But she didn't dare. His expression said the conversation was done.

Her ears pricked up at the sound of a car moving slowly down the alley. Breath froze in her lungs. Beside her, Dan stiffened. Shifted closer. He took her arm and pushed her against the wall of a building, standing in front of her.

They both let out their breaths explosively as Chief Kennedy's car came into view. Like a gentleman, Dan held the back door open for her. But she couldn't help but notice that he wouldn't meet her eyes. Nor would he stand close to her. She could feel the distance, physical and emotional, growing between them. Could almost see the wall he was putting up. After the door shut, he climbed into the front seat with the chief. The isolation washed over her.

She kept her eyes focused outside. Every movement outside had her heartbeat quickening. Were they being followed? She glanced out the back window. No other cars were visible on the street behind her. They turned onto a dirt road with an unreadable sign. As the car bounced along, she gritted her teeth. One hand braced against the ceiling to help her keep her balance.

Five minutes later, they arrived at Chief Kennedy's house. The chief led the way, and Dan stood behind her. She knew they had placed themselves to protect her. A light blinked on. She stumbled back. Dan's arm steadied her before he pulled away.

"It's all right," Chief Kennedy said. "The light's motion activated."

He quickly deactivated his security system, reactivating it once they were all inside.

"Let me go put on some coffee, then we can talk. Jace will join us after he finishes the report he's working on."

The chief left the room and an awkward silence descended. Dan got busy checking his email on his phone, but Maggie strongly suspected that he was just avoiding her. It was just as well. She had gotten too close to making another mistake.

Pain grew in her soul as she realized she had let down her guard. She had allowed herself to start to care for another man. She was such a fool. First she married a liar, then she started falling for a cop who saw her as a way to atone for past mistakes.

She was done. At least she was getting her faith back. Maybe her mom had been right all those years ago. Maggie still remembered her mom's favorite Bible verse. It was in Psalms 146:3–5, if she remembered correctly. In her mind, she repeated the verse.

*Put no trust in princes, in mere mortals powerless
to save. When they breathe their last, they return to
the earth; that day all their planning comes to nothing. Happy are those whose help is Jacob's God, whose
hope is in the Lord, their God.*

It was amazing that she still remembered that after
all these years. Almost as if God had known she would
need it someday. Huh. It was about time she took that
lesson to heart.

What had just happened?

Had he really told her all that? He hadn't let anyone
see that part of his past.

He needed to step carefully. The last thing he wanted
was to hurt her when he left. And leave he would. Any
relationship was impossible; he was too scarred, too
broken to be a good husband for any woman. He thought
of Siobhan and Rory. His throat ached as he reminded
himself he couldn't be a good father for children, either.

She would need to find someone else.

Jealousy stabbed him in the gut. No. When this case
was done, he would pack up and transfer somewhere
else. The thought of leaving his friends left him feeling
hollow. But there was no way he could stay and watch
Maggie fall in love with someone else.

Too disturbed by his train of thought, he decided he
needed to do something. Anything. He headed toward
the kitchen. Maggie followed him. The front porch light
flared to life again. A second later, a knock on the door
had him switching directions. Grabbing Maggie's hand,
he pushed her down behind the sofa, then moved to the
blinds. He peered out into the night. Blew out his breath.

Jace. He let the other man in, then the three went to find Paul in the kitchen.

Paul was on the phone when they entered. He held up a finger to tell them he would be a minute. Dan nodded. He switched his gaze to Jace, who went to lean against the counter. Paul set down the phone and both his officers watched him. He nodded at Dan and Maggie.

"That was the Pittsburgh police. They caught the woman who was searching for Maggie. She was a paid actress. She was contracted to act the part of an anxious sister. Was able to show a contract and bank statement. We haven't been able to trace the payment yet. She thought she was getting involved with some new reality TV show."

Jace snorted. Dan had to agree.

"What people'll do for a little bit of fame."

Paul grabbed his briefcase and shuffled inside it. "Ah, there it is!" He pulled out a file and handed it to Dan. "This is all the information we were able to get on Malcolm Hutchins. It seems his old boss, a man by the name of Gordon Spiles, was running a small money laundering scam at his business. Malcolm turned him in. Spiles was convicted and went to prison."

"Then why was Phil—I mean Malcolm still in danger?" Maggie blurted. Then she colored when all three officers turned her way. "Sorry. I didn't say anything. I'm just a fly on the wall."

A smile tugged at Dan's mouth against his will. Even embarrassed she was spunky.

Paul chuckled. "Quite all right, Ms. Slade. To answer your question, he would have been safe if Spiles had been the man on top. But he wasn't. He was, in fact, working for someone else. That's who we have to find."

"I think I should go visit the ex-wife. See if she knew anything," Dan said, trying not to notice as Maggie winced. "Maggie, I don't think you should come with me on this one."

Maggie appeared torn between relief and anxiety.

Paul seconded the idea. "Seeing you would only rub salt in her wounds. She might feel she could have saved him if she had stayed. Which might sound ridiculous, but that's how some people think."

Dan shot Paul a look. Was that a hidden barb against himself? No, Paul didn't appear to be saying anything more than his words implied. Nor did Jace seem to notice anything. Only Maggie seemed to hear the irony. Her eyebrows were raised and there was a definite smirk on her pretty face.

Jace stretched, yawning. "In the meantime, Mel said I should invite you all over for a late supper. Maggie, you can sleep at our house tonight."

Put on the spot, Maggie seemed to lose some of her self-confidence. She flicked her eyes toward Dan. Feeling protective, he moved over to stand next to her. He bumped his arm against hers once, just to remind her that he was on her side. Her shoulders straightened. Good. He hated to see her doubt herself.

"Sure, Jace," he answered in a casual voice. "I'd much rather eat Melanie's cooking than my own."

Not to mention Jace had put in a state-of-the-art security system in the house when he'd married Melanie. Then he'd given her a huge black Lab for her birthday. The house was safer than Dan's apartment. Not that he could take her there. It wouldn't be appropriate.

"I think I will pass—" Paul began.

"Paul," Jace cut in. "It'll just be us. Nothing formal."

What? Dan narrowed his gaze and really looked at his boss. Paul's face had gone expressionless at the invite, but now it resumed a more natural if somewhat sadder expression. Why would he be sad? Paul ate at Jace's house all the time. So did he. They always had a good time. Suddenly, he realized something. The only times he'd been present and Paul wasn't was when Jace's younger sister, Irene, and her husband, Tony, were there. Dan liked Tony. He was a fellow cop, just a couple years younger. He was outrageous and funny, very Italian. At work, he and Paul got along great. So Paul wouldn't have a reason to avoid Tony...

Oh, man. It must have been Irene he was avoiding. But why? There must be some history there.

Paul noticed him watching. "Thanks, Jace. Why don't you just put an ad in the paper that the chief of police is scared to be in the same room with your sister?"

Jace bit his lip. "Sorry, man. I just wanted you to know you were welcome. I'm sure Irene has forgiven you."

Forgiven him? This was getting interesting, but Dan felt uncomfortable getting such a personal glimpse into his friends' lives. Especially into something Paul clearly didn't want to discuss. Dan slid his eyes to Maggie. She was riveted to the conversation before them, her head tilted and her brows furrowed. She had obviously caught the undertones but didn't know enough specifics to draw an accurate conclusion.

"Can we please stop talking about it?" Paul rubbed his neck.

Okay, this he could deal with.

"Talking about what?" Dan raised an eyebrow at

Jace. "Dude, do you have any clue what he's ranting about?"

Jace played along, as Dan had known he would.

"Nah, not one. He's been under stress. Maybe it's taking its toll."

"Yeah, we better get something to eat. What did Mel make?"

"Chicken enchiladas and Spanish rice."

On cue, Dan's stomach gave a loud rumble. The three men started laughing. "Let's go."

Only then did he notice Maggie's stiff posture. Her hands were clenched at her sides and the color had leeched from her face. Her black curls made her skin appear even whiter.

"Maggie! What's wrong?"

She avoided looking at Jace and Paul. Her slender frame was shaking.

"How can I go to that house, Dan?" she hissed. "I was on the jury that put her in jail. I don't belong in her home."

She was ready to cry, Dan realized, alarmed. He put his arm around her shoulders and drew her close. "Shh, Mags. I told you, Melanie doesn't hold a grudge. Think of Jace here. He put her in jail and she still married him. Honest. I wouldn't let you go there if I thought she held you responsible or blamed you in any way."

She still wouldn't look at him. Using one knuckle, he gently edged up her chin so he could see her blue eyes. It was important that she believe him. The urge to kiss her when their eyes met took him by surprise. He tightened his grip on her shoulders for a brief moment before letting her go. Deliberately not looking at Jace and Paul, he watched her.

Finally, she straightened her shoulders and gave one quick nod. Her jaw was taut, which let him know she was still worried. But, he noted with pride, she wasn't going to let her worries stop her.

That's my girl.

Except she wasn't. And never would be.

ELEVEN

Melanie Tucker was not what Maggie had expected. Oh, she remembered the long dark hair, brown eyes and smallish stature. What she didn't remember was the beaming smile, which seemed to fill the room with warmth. Melanie radiated peace and joy. But there was also a strength about her. Here was a woman who had known sorrow but had not been controlled by it.

Her eyes stung as Melanie greeted her husband. Jace and Melanie were truly in love, and they didn't need to touch for it to show. It was in every glance and smile. Maggie shook her head. Who would have figured that these two would have ended up together, given their history?

When Dan introduced her to Melanie, Maggie decided to bite the bullet. She had learned long ago that sometimes you just needed to be blunt.

"I'm sorry that I thought you were guilty six years ago," she stated, ignoring Dan, whose jaw dropped. Hopefully Jace would catch him if he fell over. "I acted without malice, but I will totally understand if you don't want me in your home."

Melanie exchanged glances with Jace.

"This is kinda déjà vu-ish," she remarked to him. Then to the others, she said, "When I was first released, Jace's mother didn't want me in her home because she thought I was a criminal. I decided then that I would never unfairly judge another if I could help it." She walked forward and took Maggie's hands. "I hold nothing against you. You did what you were supposed to. The fault wasn't yours."

Blinking back sudden tears, Maggie nodded.

"Enough with the drama. I'm starving," Dan complained.

"Stop your whining. Dinner's ready." Taking her husband's hand, Melanie led the way to the kitchen. The table was already set. It wasn't until they were all seated around the table that Maggie realized there was one extra place setting. She raised her eyes and saw Dan was looking at the same spot.

"Um, Melanie? Are you still expecting someone?"

Something in his voice alerted Maggie to the fact that he was nervous. Melanie, however, looked serene. Maggie wasn't fooled. There was pure defiance in her eyes.

"Yes. There was someone else who wanted to meet Maggie."

Who wanted to meet her? Her stomach cramped. A tremor started deep inside. Had Melanie betrayed her? Was this a trap? Desperate, Maggie started to rise, but Dan's hand on her wrist made her pause.

"You're safe. No one would harm you here."

Easy for him to say. Or maybe not. He was looking a little tense himself.

Someone knocked on the front door. It squeaked on its hinges slightly as it was pushed open.

"Mel? Jace?"

She had never heard that male voice before. It sounded young. Dan's shoulders relaxed beside her. Whoever it was, Dan knew and was okay with him.

"We're in the kitchen," Melanie called out.

Footsteps approached the door and it swung open. A man close to her own age appeared. He was wearing a paramedic jacket. Maggie noticed his dark curly hair and his dark eyes, but what really stood out was his face. He had the same high cheekbones, straight nose and strong jawline as she had. She was looking at the male version of her own face.

As if from a distance she heard Melanie say, "Hi, Seth. Come meet your sister Maggie."

Maggie slowly rose to her feet, her eyes glued to the man who was staring back at her.

"What?" In all the drama of the past few years, it never had occurred to her that the senator's son, her half brother, would want to meet her. Sure, she'd thought about him, wondered what he was like, but had never allowed her mind to wander beyond that. Part of her had assumed he would hate her. It was incredible to think that he had wanted to meet her, as well!

But the truth was walking toward her. And he had tears in his eyes.

"Maggie," he said. Just her name. She was too shell-shocked to react when he embraced her. It was too surreal. The shock started to wear off and she pulled back. This was the son of Joe Travis. The man who had committed bigamy by marrying her mother under false pretenses. But his eyes were warm, and his open face spoke of his gentle spirit.

She grew worried she had offended him. But he only smiled, a sad and wistful smile.

"It's okay. We need to get to know each other."

A warmth at her right elbow alerted her to Dan's presence. He was letting her know that he was there. She sent him a smile to reassure him.

"I only learned about you after you had disappeared," Seth informed her. "If I had known… I always wanted a sister. I would have protected you, looked after you."

Maggie felt tears well in her eyes but blinked them back.

"I could have used a big brother."

Warmth soaking into her hair woke her. The bed in the guest bedroom was right next to the open window and sunlight was streaming in. Maggie sat up slowly and stretched to work out the kinks that the past few days had left her with. But at least something good had happened last night. A brother. Wow. A smile spread across her face. She caught a glimpse of herself in the mirror above the dresser. She looked happy. The happiness faded as she realized her babies had an uncle. But when would it be safe for them to meet him?

She had talked with Seth for an hour after dinner. He had recently lost his mother, who had been sick for years. His father had "married" her mother while still married to his. It pained Seth to know that if his mother hadn't gotten sick, his father would have left her years ago. But he put the blame squarely where it belonged— on his father rather than on Anna or Maggie. Since learning of her existence, his relationship with their father had become strained. She was sorry for Seth, although she certainly couldn't blame him. On the plus side, Seth was over the moon about gaining a sister and a niece and nephew. She also learned that Seth was the one who had put her belongings in storage. He'd never given up hoping to find her alive. They had tentatively planned to get together soon, although no details had been firmed up.

Her clothes were folded up on the chair in the corner. Melanie must have washed them. She should get dressed. Dan wanted to go through her belongings in storage to see if they could find what Phil—Malcolm— had on his old boss. Lazily, she glanced at the clock.

"Oh, my!"

Dan was picking her up at eight-thirty. It was 8:12 a.m. now. She never slept past six-thirty. Never!

Recent events apparently had left her exhausted.

After swinging her legs over the edge of the bed, her feet hit the floor and she took off to the guest bathroom, where she took the quickest shower of her life. Without even bothering to brush her wet hair, she bunched it up in a sloppy bun and jammed in several bobby pins from a drawer. Melanie *did* say she could borrow anything. She was dressed and ready by 8:25 a.m. Good. Hopefully Dan would be late and she could grab a quick bagel or a piece of toast. The aroma of coffee was drifting in the air as she stepped into the hallway, so she knew someone else was up and moving. Her old sneakers made soft shuffling noises in the hall. She walked into the kitchen.

Stopped.

Stared.

Leaning against the counter was Dan. It was a good thing she was so familiar with his strong features and casual posture as he leaned against the counter drinking coffee from a travel mug, because she might not have recognized him otherwise. Gone were the long hair

and the short beard. The man before her was sporting a
newly close-cropped hairstyle and a clean-shaven face.
Who knew his jaw was so square? Whoa.

"Hi. I'm looking for a friend of mine. His name's
Dan. Kinda quiet, sometimes cranky."

He rolled his eyes, but a grin broke over his face.
When he tilted his head back and challenged her with
his eyes, her stomach fluttered. *Get a hold of yourself,
Maggie. You have no time to go soft on a guy. Even if
he is gorgeous and has a huge hero complex.*

"Yeah, yeah. Ha-ha," he responded to her quip. "It
was time."

"I have to admit, I'd never seen a cop with long hair
before."

He dipped his head in acknowledgment.

"And I never intended to be a long-haired cop. It
just grew, and I was too lazy to cut it. But it was getting in my way."

She couldn't help herself. Moving in closer, she
rubbed her hand over his head. And grinned. It tick-
led her palm.

"It's fuzzy."

"Men do not have fuzzy hair," he growled. "It's
functional."

Maggie chuckled and removed her hand. Or at least
she meant to. As it slipped off his head, he caught it.
And then her gaze. The breath whooshed from her
lungs. She couldn't breathe.

Pulling her hand free, she broke eye contact and
grabbed the bag of bagels.

"Coward," she thought she heard.

Whipping her head around to face him, she found
him innocently reading an email on his phone.

"What?" she demanded.

"Hmm?" He put away the phone and raised a questioning brow at her. "We should head out soon. Think you can eat in the car?"

She glared at him, then finished making her breakfast in silence.

Five minutes later, they were in his car. Thankfully, not a police car. She didn't want to draw any more attention to herself than necessary. Although, judging from the recent events, it seemed as though nothing they did could keep her hidden from danger for long.

Dan swerved the car to the curb to allow a pickup truck that was driving too close to pass them. His eyes were narrowed as he watched it in his mirror. Did he suspect that it might be following them? His expression cleared as it passed them.

A shiver went down her spine. Maybe she was paranoid, but she had a feeling things would get worse before they got better.

Man, he couldn't believe all the stuff she had. How on earth could one person accumulate so much junk? Living in a myriad of foster homes and then the army had forever cured him of the need for a ton of material goods.

But Maggie? The storage unit was filled with furniture—more than necessary, in his opinion. Then there were knickknacks, boxes of cooking stuff and books. Boxes and boxes of books. Textbooks, hardbacks, paperbacks.

"You know," he commented drily, "there is such a thing as a library."

Maggie stuck her tongue out at him. He grinned. She was adorable.

"I like books."

"Yeah, I can see that."

A huge sigh erupted from her. She turned her attention to yet another box of *stuff*. "Books are like friends, but without the judgment. I can always count on them to help me escape."

He shook his head, but he understood, having heard about her childhood. Any escape would have been good.

"Ever thought of getting an e-reader?"

She frowned. "I love real books. They take up more space, but I don't mind." She cast a look around at the boxes. "I haven't had the luxury of buying books since I went into hiding."

"That reminds me, how did you have money to pay for things?"

Maggie shrugged. "Wendy paid me in cash for watching her house. Plus, the household expenses were on automatic from her account. And then there was the money…"

Her voice dwindled and her eyes grew huge. She lost color so quickly, Dan moved closer in alarm.

"Maggie? What is it? What's wrong?"

"Money," she whispered in shock. "I was using my husband's money."

Dan realized his mouth had dropped open. He shut it with a loud click.

"I think you need to explain that."

"Phillip was paranoid about money, at least I thought he was. He kept a rainy-day fund in a safety deposit box at a bank in Erie. He said it was his life savings that we could use if we were ever struggling. I assumed that he meant if we lost our jobs, since the economy wasn't doing so hot. When I ran after I saw him get shot, I drove there and opened the box. Took the money."

"How much money?"

"Twenty K."

Dan whistled. "Twenty thousand? That's not pocket change."

Maggie was shaking her head desperately. "There was more in there than just the money, Dan. I took the cash, but I left everything else."

That meant…

"The evidence is probably in that box," he exclaimed. Before she could answer, he had his phone out. "I need the number and the name on the box. And the bank location," he rapped out. As soon as he had the information, he was on the phone with Paul. His chief's normally calm drawl was taut with excitement as he promised to have the box checked out immediately. Exhilarated, Dan whirled back to Maggie. "We can probably—"

A revving engine cut him off. It was close. Too close.

The driver of the pickup truck he had let pass them earlier was gunning his engine and heading straight for them. Dan leaped over three boxes, knocking them over. He grabbed Maggie and pushed her to the back corner of the unit.

Slam!

The unit shuddered and creaked. Boxes toppled. Somewhere to the left something made of glass shattered. The truck backed up. Grabbing the mattress leaning against the back of the unit, Dan tugged and yanked with both hands. It moved, but not enough. Maggie's hands joined his and they tugged again. This time they were able to put the mattress in between them and the front of the storage unit. Just in time. The maniac in the truck made another run for them, tires squealing. Maggie screamed and buried her face in his chest. Again, the unit shuddered. The dresser slid and banged against the mattress. It was a good thing the mirror wasn't still attached to it. Bolts popped loose and the unit's door caved in. Dust swirled, making breathing difficult.

A sliver of light sliced its way through the opening made by the broken bolts. The truck slammed into the unit again. The impact sent them crashing into the wall. Maggie gasped in pain. It was then that Dan noticed the tools spilled on the floor.

"Thank You, Lord!" he uttered in gratitude. Spreading his fingers as far as they could go, he stretched out and his fingers brushed over a crowbar. Once. Twice. Got it! Gripping it firmly, he wedged it into the gap created by the missing bolts and worked it wider with all his might. The damaged storage unit creaked and groaned, but he was finally able to get a big enough hole to slide Maggie through.

"Go!" he whispered harshly, letting out a sigh of relief when she complied without argument. He wedged the hole wider, then slipped through himself, taking care to avoid the sharp edges. Why wasn't the truck still hammering at them?

He grabbed Maggie's hand and motioned for her to stay low. She nodded. They scuttled off along the back of the row of units. That was when they heard the gunshots. The maniac was shooting into the unit. Dan shoved Maggie unceremoniously behind the bushes growing beside another unit. Then, drawing his gun, he flattened himself against a wall and started to inch his way to where he had a decent view of the perp. A car door slammed. A frustrated sound escaped between

Dan's lips. He jumped out from his hiding place just in time to see the taillights disappearing around the curve. Shoving his gun back into the holster, he stalked to the front. And felt his heart drop. The entire front of the storage unit was demolished, caved in like a cereal box that had been stomped on. Holes where the bullets had entered were clearly visible. The large door, which had previously slid up and down like a garage door, had been shoved off its track. In fact, the track itself was broken off in parts. No wonder the guy had left without going in to check on them. The perp probably figured there was no way anyone could have survived that. Seeing the damage firsthand, he was awestruck that they *had* both survived relatively unharmed.

"I can't believe we're alive."

Dan jumped, then frowned. How had she sneaked up on him? "We survived because we had God on our side."

"I'm beginning to think you might be right."

It was amazing how much joy one simple statement could cause. That she wasn't skeptical at the mention of God was astounding. That she was giving consideration to his statement was humbling.

"How did he know we would be there?"

Dan looked over at Maggie. Her forehead was developing a bruise already. He winced. That had to hurt.

Picking up his cell phone, he put a quick call in to Paul. In succinct detail, he related what had happened.

"Are you and Maggie okay?"

"Yes, sir. Didn't get a license plate number on the truck, but I'm pretty sure it was following us this morning."

"My guess, whoever was paying Dennis knew we

were keeping guard over Maggie. He probably saw you with her."

"Or," Dan butted in, "maybe he saw who wasn't with her. We don't have a huge police station. Whoever this guy is, he appears to have enough money to pay for multiple spies. It wouldn't have been difficult to learn that I was the only officer unaccounted for this morning."

There was a thoughtful silence as they considered what they knew.

"It could be just a hunch," Paul pronounced each word slowly, "but it seems to me that Malcolm Hutchins got himself involved with more than a mere money laundering scheme. Something bigger is going on."

"I need to go see Hutchins's ex-wife, but it's too dangerous to take Maggie there." Dan turned away slightly when he saw Maggie's chin lift in defiance. He wouldn't allow her to sway him on this. There was too much at stake.

A thought struck him.

"Paul, don't let anyone know I called, okay? I think the only reason Maggie and I are still alive right this minute is because this guy smashed up the unit too badly to come in after us and make sure we were dead. This place is pretty out of the way, so it's feasible that you wouldn't know we were in there when this happened. Which buys us some time."

"You could be right. If we could get Maggie in here to the station without anyone knowing about it, she could hide out in my office for a few hours. If we keep the window blinds down and the door locked, no one should have any reason to suspect she's in there."

Dan hesitated, remembering the last attack. A look at Maggie's pale face strengthened his resolve.

"I don't think we should risk the police station. It's too public, even if we try to sneak her in. I could bring her to stay with Seth. He would do anything to keep her safe."

"He would, but I don't want the senator to get wind of her presence. Not yet. I don't trust him."

"He is a loose cannon, that's for sure." Dan flicked a glance at Maggie. She was attending his side of the conversation carefully, although he hoped she didn't know who Paul was talking about. She did look worried. Oh, wait. He had mentioned Seth. *Not Seth*, he mouthed at her. She relaxed.

"All we need is for Senator Travis to start using his long-lost daughter as a political maneuver," Dan continued. It was a sad statement, but the truth. The senator had a track record for his lack of compassion. In the past he had used other people's problems to help his own agenda. That was part of the reason Melanie had gone to jail. The senator had used her case to bolster his political career. *Not gonna happen this time.*

Maggie tugged at his sleeve.

"Hold on, Paul." Placing a hand over the microphone on his phone, he raised his eyebrows at Maggie.

"Seth said last night that his dad is in Ohio this week. Some kind of convention."

He smiled and nodded before addressing Paul again. "Paul? Maggie says the senator's out of town this week."

A second later he hung up. It was all set. Maggie would hang out with Seth. A carefully vetted cop would be hidden on the premises. Dan muttered a prayer under his breath for her safety and his. It was only a matter of time before the killer caught up with them again. Hopefully they'd be ready.

TWELVE

Seth was more than happy to have Maggie over. They had spent the morning doing normal brother and sister things together. Talking and laughing. Playing board games. They had even watched a movie together. About halfway through the film, Seth had fallen asleep on the couch. Maggie was hesitant to wake him. She knew he had been on call the night before and had had only three hours of sleep. She decided to occupy herself with a book from his collection of mysteries. But she couldn't focus on it. Her mind kept dwelling on Dan.

For what felt like the fiftieth time, Maggie looked at the clock on the wall. Five minutes later than the last time she had checked. With a frustrated sigh, she tossed the paperback she had been pretending to read aside and prowled around the combined dining area and living room. Seth had managed to create a warm and inviting, yet masculine environment. What was Dan's house like? Dan wasn't much about making a personal statement, she mused. She thought back to the brief glimpse she had had of his work area the one time she had been at the station. The wall next to his desk held his certifications, but nothing else. No pictures, no mementos

from friends. Not even a colorful wall calendar. It was
rather bleak. The office of an emotionally isolated man.
But he was so much more than that. Yes, he was doing
his best to keep his distance, but she had witnessed his
warmth. His sense of humor. His despair.

She shook her head. How he decorated or didn't dec-
orate his office—or his home—was nothing to her. Or
it shouldn't be. As soon as she was safe, she would collect her babies and her association with Lieutenant Dan
Willis would come to an end. That really stank.

But she knew she had no future with a man like Dan.
Not only because he had issues, but also because she
didn't want a man whose job involved danger. Did she?
Absolutely not. She had her kidlets to consider. They
deserved a father who could be certain he'd be there
for them. But since when was she searching for a father
for her children? Since never, that was when. She was a
strong, independent single mom. And that was the way
she liked it.

She was giving herself a headache over this. Slump-
ing in her chair, she closed her eyes and massaged her
temples with her fingers. She was tired, cranky, and
oh, how she missed her kids. Unbearably so. Just thinking of them made her ache. Was Rory having trouble
sleeping? He was used to her rocking him at night. And
Siobhan... Vonnie had been teething when she'd left.
Her little gums would get so red and angry looking,
and she would scream and wail until Maggie made the
pain go away.

Footsteps sounded on the porch. They seemed to
echo in the silent room. Maggie leaped from the chair
she had just sat down in and shot across the room. She
crouched down in the corner, behind another chair,

heart pounding. Her mouth was dry, so she tried to swallow. Seth opened his eyes and sat up. Frowning, he glanced around the room until his eyes came to rest on her. Upon seeing her, he gave her a tight smile and hurried from the room. She pulled her arms in tighter and bowed her head to make herself as small as possible. Briefly she closed her eyes. She should pray. Dan would. The door opened.

"Maggie?" Maggie opened her eyes and saw Chief Kennedy watching her. She straightened from her crouched position. That was when she noticed Jace and another police officer in the room.

"I'll be in the kitchen if you need me," Seth informed her from the doorway. He pulled the door closed behind him as he left. The chief moved farther into the room. "I'm sorry if I scared you. My men have gone through the safety deposit box. I thought you might be interested in seeing some of the things we found."

Relieved, Maggie surged up out of the corner to join them at the table. She didn't know how much more introspection she could handle. Shaking off the maudlin mood, she waited for the officers to continue.

"Hi, Maggie," Jace greeted her. "This is Officer Martello. He and I went to visit that bank in Erie this morning. Have a seat, and I will go through the stuff that concerns you."

Maggie understood. They were not willing to tell her everything they had found. Well, maybe she could convince Dan to tell her later. After all, she had been married to Malcolm. It was easier to call him by his real name now. Somehow, she had managed to distance herself.

Jace pulled out a large envelope. Inside were bank statements and legal documents.

"Dan told me about the twenty thousand that was in the box."

Maggie held her breath. At the time, she hadn't questioned that the money was Phillip's, therefore hers, to use. But what if it wasn't? Would she have to pay it all back?

"According to the documentation here, the money was all Malcolm's." She blew out her breath, hard. "We looked into the money he had made while working for Spiles. Pretty much everything was either used to pay off his previous debts, which he did before going to the police, or was seized under the government's asset forfeiture program. He lived very frugally after entering the Witness Protection Program. And he started making investments, very smart investments, through a third party. If I had to guess, he was planning for the day when his old boss would find him. He had pulled the money from the investments a few weeks before he was killed. And there was more than the twenty thousand." Jace showed her a statement for a bank account. Her eyes widened. That much money? It had never occurred to her that her husband had been a wealthy man.

"As soon as it is cleared, it's yours."

Dizzy, she leaned her head on her hands. She wouldn't be poor. More important than that, her children wouldn't be poor. They wouldn't be raised the same way she had been.

"Maggie? You okay?"

She nodded and cleared her clogged throat. "I'm fine. Please, continue."

"There wasn't much else."

Uh-uh. She so wasn't buying that. "You found the evidence. Right?" She turned her glare from one to the other.

Chief Kennedy entered the conversation. "I know it goes against protocol, but I think she should know a little of what we are up against."

The cop she didn't know started to protest. Chief Kennedy halted him with an upraised hand. "I will take full responsibility, Tony. But this isn't just another case. These people mean business, and they are after her. She needs to understand why they are so set on it."

Tony. She knew that name. This was the officer married to Jace's sister, Irene. Well, that explained why he was let in on the secret that she and Dan weren't dead.

"Human trafficking."

She whipped around to face Jace. Realizing her mouth was hanging open, she closed it with a click of her teeth. She didn't want to believe that the man she'd loved, the man she'd married, had been part of something so repulsive.

"Was Phillip…"

Chief Kennedy interrupted. "You don't need all the details, but I can tell you your husband was not involved in that part of the business. As best I can tell, as soon as your husband saw something that bad was going on, he decided to get out of it. He couldn't, but he tried."

Sinking into a chair, Maggie struggled to deal with the new information.

"How could he withhold that information from the FBI?" The harsh voice was barely recognizable as her own. "To turn his back on it, that's almost like, I don't know, it's like he was enabling it."

Jace leaned back against the buffet, his arms folded across his chest. "Dan told us what Robert said. The information we have, though, was dated after Malcolm was put in the Witness Protection Program. So I doubt that it's the info he withheld. If I had to guess, I would say he had a suspicion something darker was going on, but the only thing he had proof about was the money laundering. Then he kept digging into it later, after he'd entered the program."

"I'm so confused." Maggie rubbed her forehead. A nagging ache was beginning between her eyes.

"Maggie." She pulled her hands away from her eyes to meet the chief's gentle gaze. "As soon as Dan gets back, we should be able to piece together more information. Until then, I need you to be patient and lie low. It works to our advantage that the perp thinks you are dead."

"But Dan—"

"No one knows where Dan is except for us. And no one else knows about his mission today."

"But what if someone finds out?"

Chief Kennedy shook his head. "We have done a sweep of the station. Only highly trusted members of the police force have been in today. There are no bugs, his orders are not in writing and he is using a track phone to communicate. He's off the grid at the moment, and so are you."

Dan had the cab driver let him off a couple of blocks shy of Lily Hutchins's house. If anyone had realized he was still alive, he didn't want to lead them to her. He pulled his baseball cap low and hunched his shoulders to appear shorter. He adopted what he hoped was a nonchalant attitude. In reality, he was wound up so tight he felt as though he might explode at any second. Part of it was this case. Part of it was being away from Maggie. He had been mentally entangled in Maggie's whereabouts for so long it was hard to keep his perspective when he couldn't physically watch her to make sure she was safe. Not to mention his concern over the twins. Add to all that the guilt that was building inside him over Dennis's death, and he was a walking time bomb.

Digging deep, he focused on God for a moment. He didn't have the words but allowed himself to just be with the Lord as he walked.

Arriving at Lily's house, he knocked three times on the door. The sound was loud, sharp.

A minute later, he heard a clicking sound inside. Heels. Who wore high heels inside the house? The thought had barely formed when the door swung open and he was face-to-face with a woman who could have stepped off a magazine cover. Tall, elegant, with flowing gold hair and crystal blue eyes. Her skin was flawless—until you noticed the angry red scar running along the left side.

Discreetly pulling out his badge, Dan held it close to his chest and flashed it so she could see it, but anyone passing by couldn't. The only sign she gave of being surprised was the stiffening of her spine. Although her eyes darted around, making sure they were alone.

"Mrs. Hutchins," he began.

"I go by Lily Klemz now," she informed him, her eyes wary. He recognized her maiden name.

"Of course. Ms. Klemz, I need to speak with you. May I come in?"

She stood aside and motioned him inside with her head, quickly shutting and bolting the door behind him.

When she faced him again, he saw it. The terror that she was trying to hide. It was in the way she folded her arms so close against her body.

"What do you want? Is this about my worthless ex-husband?" she hissed at him.

"Yes and no. Ms. Klemz, were you aware that Malcolm had entered the Witness Protection Program under an assumed name?"

"Not until the feds showed up at my door a year and a half ago to tell me he was dead. Before that, I hadn't seen him since I left him."

He needed to tread lightly here. Bringing up her ex-husband's second wife could be tricky. It was a long shot, but he needed to know what she knew.

"How much did you know about his former job?"

She seethed. "I knew nothing about it. But that doesn't matter, does it? I was innocent, and still I have police and feds questioning me, and his old work associates harassing me—"

Whoa. What?

"Hold on. What do you mean, his old associates harassed you? Have you been in contact with them? Any names and details you could give me—"

"Names! What, you think they'd leave their cards? 'Yes, hi, I'm one of your ex's pals who works in an illegal business'?" She laughed, a chilling, ugly cackle completely devoid of humor. "All they left me with was this scar." A trembling finger pointed to her face.

Pity and sorrow grew in his heart.

"Did you report it?"

She sneered. "Yes, but the police had no leads. Nothing they could prove. The business used as a front that initially hired Malcolm had already shut down. No one was saying anything more."

Great. He'd come all this way, and it was another dead end.

"There is one thing, though. One thing that struck me as odd at the time." She paused and uncertainty washed over her expression.

"Yes? Ms. Klemz, whatever it is, you need to tell me. No matter how small it may seem."

She bit her lip. He waited, forcing down his impatience.

"After Malcolm disappeared, a man came looking for him. He said he and Malcolm used to go to school together, and he was trying to reconnect. I didn't believe him, not for a second, and was only too glad to tell him that I had no idea where my lying ex was. I forgot about it for a long time. Then months later, I opened the newspaper to see this man's face staring out at me. He was some sort of reporter or something who had been killed."

"Was his name Brandon Steel?"

Her eyes widened. "Yes."

Dan crept into his apartment as quietly as possible. Fortunately, most of the other tenants were already at work. Booting up his computer, he started researching Brandon Steel. And came up with some surprising facts. A little more research and a few phone calls, and a different picture began to evolve.

Standing up to stretch, he noticed the time. Wow. He had sat at the computer for over an hour. Maggie must be going stir-crazy at Seth's house. He would go get her soon. Although he still wasn't sure what the game plan was. His grumbling stomach reminded him he hadn't had lunch. He put together a quick ham and cheese sandwich. He ate standing up by the sink, then chugged down a glass of water. Out of the corner of his eye he saw a movement. Whirling, he just managed to dodge the baseball bat swinging toward his head. It bounced off his shoulder instead. Pain lanced through him, but he ignored it. He zeroed in on the man before him, noting the knit cap and unshaved jaw.

His attacker screamed, a shout of pure frustration, raised the bat above his head and swung again. This time Dan was ready for him. He grabbed the bat and yanked it out of his hands before tossing it aside. It clanged against the table. Then he attacked. It turned out his opponent wasn't much of a fighter when it came to hand-to-hand combat.

Dan fought to hold himself in control. He easily subdued the intruder. His jacket was hanging on the back of a chair. He swiped the handcuffs he always carried with him and restrained the other man. What he really wanted to do was pound him to a pulp. All the problems of the past few days were catching up with him. This guy had no clue how close he was to becoming a human punching bag. Dan reined in his emotions. There was too much at stake to lose it now.

He recited the Miranda rights while he grabbed his cell phone off the counter. Not the track phone, because, really, it was obvious he was no longer off the grid. He shot a quick text to Paul. He needed to know Maggie was in danger. Paul responded almost immediately that Jace was on his way in a cruiser.

Good. If he was honest, he had mixed feelings about

having his cover blown. It gnawed at him to have to hide, to rely on secrecy. Too many variables could go wrong. On the other hand, Maggie's safety was compromised.

Giving the intruder his most obnoxious smirk, he remarked, "Not so brave without a bat, huh?"

An angry snarl twisted the man's face. "I can't believe you didn't die this morning."

"Ah, so it was you in the truck. Your driving skills are questionable."

"You think you're safe? You think that chick you're hiding is out of danger?" He laughed. "She won't be safe…ever. My boss is sure she has something her hubby stole. And he has enough money to send people after her every day for the next ten years."

Without any memory of how he got there, Dan was across the room. His hands trembled with the urge to shake the audacity out of him. Clenching his fists, he shoved his face close to the other man's, ignoring the stench of chewing tobacco and sweat.

"Is this guy worth going to jail for three counts of attempted murder?"

A gleam of panic entered the other man's eyes. He probably hadn't counted on Dan living long enough to arrest him. The gleam disappeared. The man smirked back, although it appeared to be forced.

"I'd rather be in jail with my boss's backing to protect me than in Maggie's shoes. How safe do you think your little girlfriend will be when she reads today's newspaper?"

Huh? Backing away, Dan held up a hand, warning his prisoner to stay where he was. He pulled his smartphone out of his pocket and called up the web address for the local newspaper, careful to keep one eye on the man standing a few feet away.

Ice sloshed through his veins as the front page came into view.

Local Woman Found Alive After More Than a Year

Smiling up at him from his phone was an image of a young woman. It was several years old, but he would know that face anywhere. It was Maggie. And the story below sent dread coursing through him. The reporter somehow had found out about the twins and Anna. The story didn't come out and say they were being hidden. No, it made it seem as though Maggie's mother was merely becoming acquainted with her grandchildren. But the facts were undeniable. Someone had found out about them. Now they were in danger, too.

THIRTEEN

Maggie paced the confines of Melanie's kitchen, alternating between frustration and anger. It seemed all she had done lately was wait. How she hated being forced to wait when people she cared about were in danger! Every now and again she would stop and mutter a prayer. It felt awkward, but she was desperate to do anything she could to get her babies back safe. And her mother. She knew if any harm came to her children it would mean her mother had been incapacitated or worse.

Shouldn't she have heard something by now? Jace and Dan had left hours ago! The sun had set, and she could see a few stars out the window. In the background, she could hear the murmur of voices as Melanie and Jace's sister, Irene, chatted in the next room.

Dan's phone call had caused a flurry of activity. Melanie and Irene had gone out to Seth's house to pick her up and bring her back to the house, while Jace and Dan had lit out of there, the siren blaring on the cruiser. Paul had headed into the station. He needed to plug a leak, he had stated darkly, and he wouldn't leave the station until it was done. Maggie wasn't surprised. The chief of police was very charming, but she strongly suspected it was a facade to hide a very lonely man. It didn't seem as though he had anyone to rush home to.

Reverting to a habit she'd had since childhood, Maggie started talking to herself. In Gaelic. Slipping into the tongue she had learned from her grandmother had always brought her comfort, as if her grandmother were close by.

"If something were wrong, I would have heard. Dan wouldn't keep me in suspense. Or maybe something did go wrong and he just wants to tell me in person. No, he wouldn't do that. They're fine. Everyone's fine." Absently, she picked up the dish towel from the counter and began to swish it back and forth in front of her.

A car pulled into the driveway. Dropping the towel, she charged through the kitchen door and beat Melanie to the front entrance. The first cruiser was followed by a second. Maggie's gaze was riveted to the cars as the front doors opened. The two officers who had stayed with her family exited the first vehicle. Jace and Dan exited the second. She could see movement in the backseat. Dan opened the passenger-side door and her mother stepped out.

With a cry, Maggie dashed down the steps to the vehicle. She tore open the back door and tried to unfasten Rory's car seat restraints with hands that trembled. Tears filled her eyes. Everything around her grew blurry. She blinked them back. Both children started wailing and reaching toward their mother. Strong hands brushed her aside gently. Dan undid Rory's seat restraints and handed the squirming little boy to her. No sooner did she have him than his chubby arms were holding on to her for dear life, his hands fisted in her hair. She didn't care. It felt like the first time she could fully breathe since she'd left them. On the other side of the car, Siobhan's wails grew in volume.

Maggie gave a watery chuckle. "Someone's not happy. Mom, give her to me, please."

Without a word, Anna walked over and deposited the little girl in Maggie's other arm. Anna kissed Maggie's cheek and rubbed her back. And was thanked with a smile. Maggie spread kisses and tears all over her children's faces. She strongly suspected their grandmother had been spoiling them, as their faces were decidedly sticky. She wasn't about to complain, though.

"Hey, Mags." Dan's soft voice snagged her attention. "Can we move this party inside? We have lots to discuss, and I for one would feel better if you weren't so out in the open."

"Yeah, good idea." When he held out his arms to take one of the twins, though, she hesitated. It seemed too soon to give either of them up, even though she knew it would be for only a minute or two.

"You walk. Your mom and I will guide you." He put his hands on her left shoulder and elbow. Anna mimicked his position on the right side. It took some fancy maneuvering, but soon the small group had moved into the house. Once they were all inside, Melanie activated the alarm system on the wall.

"We got that system set up soon after Melanie moved back in here," Jace informed her. Maggie could read between the lines. After Melanie had been released from prison. "I wasn't comfortable with how isolated this place was. Paul had a similar system set up at my mom's house."

There was more to the story than that. Mel had already told her about the threats to her life after she had been released. This time when the familiar tinge of guilt tried to edge itself in, Maggie kicked it to the curb. She couldn't live her life second-guessing decisions she had made in good faith. Especially since Melanie herself seemed to hold no grudges.

It took some effort, but Maggie managed to settle herself and her giddy twins on the floor. They were very clingy, which came as no surprise to her. They had never been out of her care that long before. What did surprise her was that Dan seated himself on the floor with them. He scooted next to her and took a clambering Siobhan up onto his lap. Her eyes widened when her daughter laughed and settled in. She glanced up just in time to catch the amused look that flashed between Jace and Melanie.

Undeterred by the unprofessional position he was in, Dan started his briefing. It began fairly straightforward. And then it took an unexpected twist.

"It would appear that Malcolm's brother had his story wrong."

Maggie felt as if her heart were lodged in her throat.

"Wrong about what? That his brother died because of me?"

She felt the sudden stillness in the room. Even Dan paused.

"He didn't die because he met you," he declared finally. "In fact, chances are good that he used you. At least in the beginning."

She pressed her lips together. Used her?

"Used me? How?" She winced. Her voice had a sharper edge than she had intended. Rory whimpered. She soothed him with a gentle cuddle, never taking her eyes off Dan.

"He and Steel had been working together for months. They had gone to school together. Steel was trying to make a name for himself. I talked with some of his old coworkers and buddies. One of them happened to over- hear an intense argument between them right before Hutchins ended their association. It seems Steel had heard of what had gone down with Spiles's business and had tracked Hutchins down. Hutchins had kept some records from the feds, just like his brother said, but nothing that was clearly illegal. He had a partner- ship with Steel, who would do some digging to get to the dirt. It was beneficial for both of them. Steel got fodder for his column and made a name for himself, and Hutchins was able to send anonymous tips to the police, which—according to Steel's crony—he did sev- eral times. Steel was very good at digging. He managed to find information on several corrupt businesses in that manner. Then he hit pay dirt. We were right. The money laundering business was only a small part of what was going on."

"Human trafficking?" *Please, say no.*

Dan nodded, his face weary. "Yeah. I'm afraid so. Steel needed Hutchins but couldn't take the chance of being seen with him. You worked at the same paper, so you presented Hutchins with a solid justification for hanging around."

A dull ache built up inside. So, everything about her marriage had been built on a lie. Including the love she had been so sure she had shared with her husband.

"Mags, don't look like that."

Look like what? As if her world had been torn apart—again? As if betrayal was ripping her heart out?

A warm, masculine hand touched her chin, tipping

her face up. Dan's eyes were worried. "I think Malcolm really had loved you in the end. His association with Steel was finished months before he married you. Months before Steel wrote that column that got him killed, even. The man I talked to said that in the argument he overheard, Malcolm was concerned about putting his girl in danger. I'm guessing that Malcolm probably carried the zip drive with him out of fear that it might fall into the wrong hands if he didn't guard it personally. If he dropped it while visiting you, it's possible that Steel found it and was unable to resist the temptation. Then he replaced it among your belongings."

"So many lies," Maggie whispered.

"I know, Maggie. But Malcolm, he could have just walked away from you. Instead, he stayed. Married you. Unfortunately, it appears that Steel got careless, or greedy, and alerted the wrong people to how he had gotten his leads. The very people that Hutchins was hiding from."

Drawing in a deep breath, Maggie did her best to shove her pain aside. She couldn't deal with it now, not with so many people watching her. Stiffening her spine, she resolved to remain strong. She had to.

"So, who was in charge of the human trafficking? Did you find him?"

Dan hesitated. Uh-oh. That meant she wasn't going to like his answer.

"We know who it is. A man named Gary Chambers." Dan paused, rubbing his face. "He definitely has enough money and resources to keep sending people after you. My guess is that he wants you dead because he knows you have connections with the press. And he has no idea how much, or how little, Hutchins told you. You are a complication he can't afford."

Maggie swallowed. "So where is he?"

"We can't find him. He disappeared about the same time I found you."

The color seeped from her already-pale face. Dan held out an arm, ready to catch her if she fainted. She swayed but leaned her back against the couch. Her eyes took on a fierce glint, and a surge of pride took him unawares. She was clearly terrified, but she wasn't about to give in to her fear. He knew her well enough to know that she was a fighter.

"We will find him, Maggie," he promised her, although he knew better. Who could tell what would happen? But he was determined that he wouldn't rest until this beautiful woman and her children were safe. "There are bulletins out with his description. And even if he is in disguise, we'll be on the lookout for anything strange."

"I know you will." The confidence in her voice, in the look she leveled at him, shook him to the core. What had he ever done to deserve such faith?

"Maggie—" He had no idea what he had planned on saying. Whatever it was, he never got the chance. The alarm started shrieking as a car squealed into the driveway. A car door slammed. Dan put the child on his lap on the floor with her mother. He stood, one hand loosely covering the gun at his waist. He was aware of Jace, Olsen and Thompson adopting similar postures.

Footsteps pounded on the porch. Jace peered out the window, then unlocked the front door and opened it. Seth ran into the room, his eyes wild as he searched the occupants. He visibly relaxed when he saw Maggie. A louder wail started. Siobhan. Rory whimpered.

Jace punched in a quick code in the box on the wall. The alarm stopped. The phone rang a second later. Rolling his eyes, Jace informed the person on the other end that there was no emergency.

"At least you know it works, dude," Dan murmured, but his attention was on the drama before him. Seth was really rattled. As far as he could tell, the younger man had seen the newspaper article and put two and two together. He had rushed over to see for himself that his newfound sister was fine. And she was. But now he was also laying eyes on his niece and nephew for the first time. And Anna. His eyes widened. Dan suspected Seth had realized who she was, because his eyes kept darting between Anna and Maggie. Clearly, she was Maggie's mother. And the woman his father had cheated on his late mother with. That had to hurt. Especially so close to her death. He was pretty sure Maggie had come to the same conclusion, because her expression was soft and sympathetic.

Man, he felt bad for the guy. Sure, Seth had been a little cocky when he'd met him, but still, he was a good man—who appeared shell-shocked at the moment. He was polite to Anna, but his discomfort was obvious. As was his instant fascination with Siobhan and Rory.

Well, who could blame the man? The twins were both as cute as buttons. Not to mention spunky. Just like their mother. Dan let his eyes fall on Maggie and felt his chest tighten. *Lord, help me get her out of this mess safely.*

Four police radios crackled to life. The dispatcher's voice was amplified as it flowed from them. All four officers straightened and a grim silence met the news that a tractor trailer had overturned on I-79, becoming the catalyst for a major seven-car pile-up. Hazmat had been called, too, which could mean hazardous chemicals were leaking from the toppled rig.

Dan and Jace exchanged "what now?" glances. Neither was keen to leave the women and children when there was a high probability that another hired killer was on his way to silence Maggie. They really didn't have a choice, though. They were on duty.

"You have to stay here, Mags. If you keep the alarm on, it will let you know if so much as a cat enters the yard."

He could tell by the way her mouth tightened that she didn't like the idea of being stranded again. Despite her displeasure, she nodded. Some of the tension melted out of his shoulders. He hadn't realized just how concerned he was.

"Melly, I'm thinking it would be a good idea if you and Irene stayed, too," Jace murmured to his wife. "I'm not comfortable with this whole situation."

"I'll stay here with them until you guys get back," Seth offered. "I'm off the clock until tomorrow morning."

"Thanks, dude."

Dan held out a hand, and Seth shook it. There were few men besides Jace and Paul whom he would trust to watch the woman he loved...

What? He didn't love Maggie, couldn't love her. But even as denial flared in his brain, his heart clutched that word and held on tight. It was no use. He had done the one thing he had sworn to never do. He was in love with Maggie Slade.

Now what?

FOURTEEN

Dan tipped his head back and drained about half a bottle of water. The past five and a half hours dealing with the car wrecks had been grim. Most of the passengers had been treated and released at the scene, although two had to be transported to the hospital, and one young man had been airlifted to Pittsburgh. Dan and Jace both had sent up a prayer for him as the helicopter lifted, sending debris blowing in its wake. The driver of the tractor trailer was dead. He apparently had suffered a heart attack while driving.

Exhausted, Dan poured some of the water over his head, then wiped off the water streaming down his face with a paper towel. It had to be going on one in the morning now. Soft footsteps echoed behind him. Jace moved beside him.

"You're not going to like this."

"What?" He planted his narrow-eyed gaze firmly on Jace.

"Just keep in mind that this doesn't make me happy, either."

"Just spit it out, man. I really just want to check in on Maggie, then grab a few hours of sleep." He didn't think he'd be able to actually talk to Maggie. It was the middle of the night. He did hope that he could follow Jace home and crash on his couch. His apartment was out of the question at the moment. Too far away from Maggie. He'd never sleep. A red flag went up in his mind when his friend didn't respond. Jace's face grew even longer. He crossed his arms over his chest. No. Just no. Paul wouldn't, would he? Yes, of course he would. Paul was all about following procedure.

"We are supposed to report to the station for a briefing as soon as we are done here."

"Seriously? Does he have any idea how long I have been on duty?" Dan really hated that he sounded like a whiny kid, but come on. How many hours straight could a man work before it took its toll? However many, he felt he'd reached it three hours back.

But the chief's orders were the chief's orders. So half an hour later he was sitting in a crowded conference room as Paul gave an update on Chambers's whereabouts. He tried to tell himself he was pleased that the man had been spotted, that they had an idea of his current location, but his blood ran cold as images of Chambers going through tollbooths in Ohio were projected on the screen. Mere hours from their position. Whatever doubt he had melted away, leaving a chill in its wake. The man was coming for Maggie.

"Sir, how is it he hasn't been picked up yet?" one of the younger officers queried.

Good question. He raised an eyebrow at Paul.

"You know how these toll roads work, Jackson. Every vehicle that comes through gets captured on camera. Hardly anyone even questions it anymore. But when we sent out the photo and description of Chambers, one of the second-shift workers recalled his face. We had the security cameras checked and found a match. He came through on the turnpike around 8:00 p.m., which means—"

Dan stood abruptly. Every hair on the back of his neck was standing on end.

"Which means he could already be here."

Paul nodded. "Yes, he could already be here."

"Then we need to get back to Jace's house, sir."

Jace's cell phone chirped, signaling that he was receiving a text. A text in the middle of the night was never good. Dan tapped his fist against his thigh, just barely holding back from demanding to know what the text said. His level of anxiety grew when Jace gasped and shot him a frantic glance before tapping out a reply.

"What was that look for? What's the problem? Jace! What's goin' on?"

"Would you just chill?" Jace tossed back. "I'm trying to figure that out, too. Mel sent me a text that she was driving Maggie to the hospital. She… Hold on." He stopped speaking when his phone chirped again. Dan was ready to crawl out of his skin. What could possibly be taking so long?

"Okay, so it seems that Rory woke up screaming, running a temperature of one hundred and four degrees. He was in pain, and Maggie insisted on going to the ER."

"Poor kid," Paul sympathized. Murmurs of agreement filled the room. Paul indicated that the meeting was over, and the tired officers rose to file out of the office.

"If you'll take me to the hospital, I can collect my wife, then you can wait for Maggie. Come by my place when you're done. You can crash for a few hours at least."

Was nothing ever simple? A yawn surprised him, and he responded with a weary nod. On the way to the car Jace sent a text to his wife. She immediately sent a response. Dan watched with alarm as Jace attempted to walk and text simultaneously.

"At least wait until we're in the car," he chided. "I'm too done in to deal with you if you trip and break your leg."

"I won't—" Jace tripped over the curb, stumbling into Dan as he struggled to regain his balance.

"Told ya."

He grinned to himself as his sheepish friend tucked his phone back in his pocket.

"I'll drive. You can continue your conversation."

The trip to the hospital seemed to take forever. He tapped his fingers against the steering wheel as they waited at yet another red light. They had caught all the red lights. Every. Single. One.

"You could use your siren," his friend suggested.

He was tempted.

"We're almost there."

Jace snorted. "Almost only counts in horseshoes. Use the siren. Just so I don't need to put up with you in a bad mood any longer."

Dan resisted the impulse for another five seconds. But the idea of Maggie sitting in the waiting room, worried and out in the open, got to him. He reached out and flipped the switch. The siren blared. The car in front of him pulled over to let him pass.

At the hospital, he strode inside, his head turning as his eyes searched for a head of black curly hair.

A shriek had him whirling to the left. His heart lurched at the desperation etched across Maggie's pale face. Little Rory screamed and arched his back, his face red and streaked with tears. Pivoting on his heel, Dan moved to them. In his peripheral vision, he could see Melanie give him a slight wave as he approached. He dipped his head in response, all his attention on the woman and child in front of him.

"Mags."

Maggie couldn't remember ever being as happy to hear a voice as she was when Dan called her name. Only a handful of people were in the waiting room. Rory had slept for a few minutes here and there, but for the most part he had been shrieking nonstop for the past two hours. She was at her wit's end.

"I'm so glad you're here."

Had she really just blurted that out? Yeah, judging by the smirk on his face, she had. She could feel warmth climbing her face. His smile slipped out of sight as he turned his attention to her son. Concern creased his forehead and shadowed his gray eyes. He reached out and gently took the little boy from her.

"Hey, buddy," he crooned. "I hear you're not feeling well."

The baby gulped and sniffed. His screams turned into whimpers for a couple seconds before resuming. Maggie half expected Dan to hand the child back to her. Instead, he cuddled the baby closer and began to walk in the waiting room, talking softly into the boy's ear. Eyes followed his progress around the room. Maggie couldn't help but notice the smiles aimed at him. He looked like any other father comforting his son.

Father! What an odd thought to have. She barely knew the man. True, she liked what she knew, but her discernment regarding character, especially in men, was questionable. Her lips mashed together as she thought of Malcolm. She forced herself to use his real name. Granted, he had reasons for his duplicity, but to leave her so totally in the dark? Especially when he knew the danger he'd put her in by getting involved with her? That was unforgivable.

Unforgivable?

Uneasily, she thought about the faith she had abandoned and was now tentatively trying to get in touch with again. She might have forgotten many things, but one thing she did remember was her grandmother insisting she learn the Lord's Prayer and take it to heart. The line "Forgive us our trespasses as we forgive those who trespass against us" stood out in her mind now like a neon sign. Because she hadn't forgiven those who had harmed her in the past. Not her late husband. Not her birth father. And certainly not her stepfather. Was she even supposed to forgive him after what he had done? Surely not. But her mind flashed to Jesus on the cross. He openly forgave those who *killed* Him.

Please help me, God. Please teach me to forgive.

A quiet sense of God's presence touched her heart. No sudden fanfare or fireworks. Just a gently soothing peace washing over her. She knew she had a long way to go, and her struggle to forgive was still present. A small part of her wanted to hold on to her anger. But she felt that God had started the process of healing her soul.

"Hey, Mags. You okay?"

Startled, she lifted her face to see Dan standing over her, his eyes soft and questioning. A grin slowly spread across her face. Rory had fallen to sleep on his shoulder and was drooling on his shirt. Dan followed her gaze and rolled his eyes. A small smile slipped out, though, so she knew he wasn't annoyed. In fact, a stillness seemed to grip him before he placed an almost-reverent kiss on the toddler's head.

A choking sensation seized her. This beautiful, tormented man had caught her unawares. How many times had she promised herself that she would never fall in love again? Yet he had managed to slide right past her guard.

But how could she love someone who was even more broken than she? What kind of future was possible for them?

"Slade?"

Relieved, she stood quickly. Whoever said self-examination was good for the soul? She didn't intend to examine her feelings for Dan for a long time, if ever.

They were led back to a curtained-off cubicle. Maggie kept turning to look back over her shoulder to make sure Dan was still following. Each time, he nodded. It was silly, she knew, but she felt the need to assure herself of his presence. She hated feeling so vulnerable.

Conversation was stilted as they waited for the ER doctor to arrive. After a few minutes, it dwindled to nothing. Dan seemed to understand that she was too scattered to talk. He moved from where he had been leaning against the wall and pulled the single chair in the cubicle closer to the narrow bed, where she sat with Rory. Gratefully, she gripped his hand when he reached out to her. He winced, shooting a glance to their intertwined fingers. She gasped and started to pull away. He held on tighter. When she ceased trying to pull away, he ran his free hand up and down her arm.

"It's okay, Maggie. I'm here. Hold on to me if you want. As hard as you want. I can take it."

Maggie thought it was both macho and sweet. So like Dan. She gave in and allowed herself the comfort of holding on to another person for a change, instead of keeping her worries to herself.

A swoosh of curtain announced the arrival of the doctor. He was young and brisk, barely making eye contact as he tapped out notes on his laptop. Dan made a sound that was very close to a growl. Maggie flashed her eyes at him, shocked. He was scowling at the doctor, who took absolutely no notice of him.

After finishing whatever it was he had been typing, the doctor lifted his head and sent a distracted smile to Maggie. A smile that froze and withered as it was turned on Dan. Suddenly, he was all business. In a remarkably short time, Rory was diagnosed with a double ear infection, a prescription was written and they were discharged with enough antibiotics to last until the pharmacy opened.

"It never ceases to amaze me that I can wait for hours for a five-minute consultation," she remarked as she carried a now-sleeping Rory out of the emergency room.

"Tonight was busier than usual."

She remembered something. "By the way, you were sort of rude in there. Intimidating that poor young doctor."

He snorted. "I get irritated when people forget that the people they serve are *people* and not just statistics. I could see that to him you were just another case. He didn't even notice that you were worried and wanted some reassurance. Here, let me take him." Dan lifted the child from her arms and held him securely curled against his chest as the security doors slid open. "I told Jace to transfer Rory's car seat to my car before he took Melanie home."

Maggie laughed. "I completely forgot about his car seat. What a great mother I am!"

"You *are* a great mother. Tonight you are just a very worried and sleep-deprived mom."

She ducked her head, pleased and shy at the same time. A smile tugged at her lips. It meant a lot to hear he thought she was a great mother. It was astounding how much it meant.

Outside, the sky glowed with pink and purple hues as the sun rose. Lifting his chin, he drew in a deep breath. Maggie copied the action, letting the cool air revive her.

"I love this time of day." Maggie sighed, a contented little sound.

He smiled. "I do, too. Although, I'm probably gonna be dragging today. I didn't get a wink of sleep last night."

Guilt overrode her delight with the sunrise.

"I'm sorry, Dan. It should have occurred to me that you would be exhausted," she mourned. "Why didn't you say something? Surely we could have found some other way to protect me so you could have rested."

In the middle of the parking lot, Dan stopped. He dipped his head and gave her a stern glance. Her heart tripped. Seeing him there, so fierce even as he held her son so gently, she thought she had never seen anything more beautiful.

"I wanted to be here with you, Mags. Being here for you tonight was worth every second of missed sleep.

Even if I yawn all day, I will be happy that I was able to help you and Rory at the hospital."

Touched, she smiled as warmth filled her chest.

"Thanks. It meant so much that you were there."

Electricity built between them. One of these times they'd see actual sparks.

A sudden blast of music shattered the moment. Dan exclaimed and handed Rory back to Maggie. He patted his pockets until he found his cell phone. The ringtone ceased abruptly as he jabbed a button with his finger.

"Willis."

As she watched, his face changed. He looked every inch a cop.

"Too coincidental. Is everyone all right? Keep me informed."

Lips pursed, Dan seemed to forget she was even present. He replaced his phone, still wearing that look of concentration.

"Hey," she called softly, reminding him of her presence. "What's going on? What's too coincidental?"

"That was Jace. He woke up early and realized the power was out. And the phones. That means the security system was off. He's checking on everyone now—"

His phone rang again. This time he answered it immediately. Whatever reassurance he had been about to offer died. Dread curled up inside her. She tensed. Rory whimpered in his sleep as her grip tightened on him.

"Come on. We have to hurry." He placed a warm hand on the small of her back to hurry her along. "Your mother's missing."

FIFTEEN

Dan couldn't remember the last time he had used his siren this many times within a twenty-four-hour period. But use it he did. Every time he looked at Maggie's tense figure sitting beside him, he could see anguish pouring from every inch of her. Nothing he said could comfort her, so he limited himself to reaching over and grabbing her hand, giving it a firm squeeze. He was about to withdraw it when she squeezed back. Hard. That woman had more strength in her hands than one would think.

The wires for the power lines had been damaged. Who knew what had been used. The damage had been enough to throw all four houses on the road into complete darkness during the night. Whoever had cut them, though, apparently hadn't cared about the consequences. He had wanted Maggie. It had to have been Chambers, or one of his hired men. Had to have been.

"Why my mom? She had nothing to do with this."

He slid a glance at Maggie. She was so pale. Should he tell her his opinion? But how could he keep it from her? He knew her well enough to know she wouldn't appreciate it if she felt he were protecting her by keeping something from her, even if it was only speculation.

"My guess… My guess is it was totally dark with no electricity. Even with the moon, he wouldn't have had a clear view. He was looking for a woman with dark curly hair and thought your mom was you."

A minute ago she had been pale. Now she appeared bloodless.

"He thought she was me." It was not a question. The monotone quality of her voice sent shivers of concern darting through him.

"Maggie? Mags, we'll be to the house in five minutes. Jace and Tony are already searching. Miles— Officer Olsen—and Seth are staying with the others. I will join Jace, and we will do everything we can to get your mom back. I promise."

He hated that he couldn't promise to get her back safe, or even alive, but no matter what, he would never lie to Maggie. She deserved the truth.

He made it to the house in three minutes. Maggie was out of the car the second he unlocked the doors. She had Rory released from his car seat and was heading at a fast clip toward the house. He leaped from the driver's seat and shut his door, wincing as it slammed. Oops. Hadn't meant to shut it that hard. Not that anyone in the house would be asleep. In three jogging strides he caught up to her. She didn't even pause but kept trotting toward the house. The sharp angle of her jaw showed it was clenched.

Seth was seated on the porch swing. He stood slowly and watched them approach with an expression of crushing guilt on his face. Oh, yeah. He had stayed to protect the women and children. If the situation hadn't been so serious, Dan might have tossed a sarcastic comment about how well that had worked out. But Jace had been there, too. And Anna still had been taken. The situation couldn't have been prevented, not without prior warning as to Chambers's plans.

As soon as Maggie was in reach, Seth hugged her and Rory tight. He bent his head, laying it on top of his sister's. The morning sun highlighted a large bruise forming on the side of his forehead. Dan narrowed his eyes. Took a step closer. That hadn't been there earlier, had it?

"What happened to your head?"

Seth sighed, stepping back from Maggie.

"I woke up hungry and decided to get myself a snack. That's when I noticed the power was out. I grabbed my phone because it has a flashlight app. I was on my way to the kitchen when I heard a noise. I went to investigate… I know," he said, holding up a hand when Dan opened his mouth, "I should have notified Jace instead of going myself. Hindsight and all that. Anyway, someone hit me on the head. Not sure with what. Knocked me out."

"Why aren't you at the hospital?" His voice was sharp. He regretted that when Maggie flinched. "Sorry. I shouldn't have snapped. But the question stands."

"I'm a paramedic. I know I have a concussion. It'll still be there later. But I couldn't leave without seeing my sister. And telling her I'm sorry that I failed."

Maggie's blue eyes widened. It seemed she hadn't reached the same conclusion.

A voice came from the doorway. "If you failed, Travis, then so did I."

When was the last time he had seen Jace that tired? Probably months ago when the psychos who had framed Melanie kidnapped her. He jerked his head back toward the inside of the house.

"Tony and Miles are processing the scene."

Where was everyone else? They were supposed to evacuate the scene before they processed it.

"No offense, Seth, but why are you still here? The scene should have been evacuated."

"I was part of the scene, right? I've got a crime scene right on my head." A cocky grin slid across Seth's face. It was halfhearted, but it was still a grin. "Besides, I couldn't move without getting dizzy. And anyways, I wasn't inside. I came outside as soon as I was able to."

"Siobhan?" Her hand went to her throat. "Seth, where's my baby?"

"She, Mel and Irene were all taken to the police station," Jace answered for him. "Both for their protection and so that Mel and Irene could give statements. They only left a little bit ago."

She whirled to face Dan. He already knew what she wanted. Had his keys in his hands.

"Come on. I'll take you to the station." Jace had to stay and oversee the guys processing the scene. As the officer in charge, he couldn't leave until the job was done.

She nodded. Turned to her brother. "Seth?"

"You go. I need to clean up and get to work."

Without another word, she hurried back to the car. Dan found himself in the rare predicament of working to keep up with her. Rory was safely back in his car seat and Maggie had already buckled herself in when he sat down in the driver's seat. He offered up a quick prayer that he would be able to remain alert. Right now, adrenaline was keeping him going. Sooner or later, though, he would crash.

Putting the car in Reverse, he rotated the wheel to

spin the car around in the yard. Stopped. Peered closer. He jammed the car into Park and threw open the door.

"Stay in the car," he ordered. He didn't wait to see if she would listen. There was no time.

"Jace!"

The other officer bolted out of the house at his bellow.

"You need to see this."

Together the two men squatted down and examined the substance darkening the gravel on the driveway. Dan pointed. There. Another spot. Smaller. Slowly, they moved from spot to spot. There were nine in all. Nine that could be tracked from the driveway to the back kitchen door. Opening the screen door, there was a smear on the lower white panel. A red smear. Blood.

It would be tested, but he had a sinking feeling it would be Anna's. She was injured. Or worse.

Maggie stuck her head out the car window in the hope she would be able to see better. Nothing. She looked at the clock on the dashboard. Fifteen minutes. They had been gone for fifteen minutes.

Where had they gone? And why? She had strained to watch as the men examined something on the driveway, then moved slowly back toward the house. She felt like a pop bottle that had been shaken. Pressure was building up inside her. Soon she would be ready to burst.

She itched to go after Dan. To see what he had spotted that had caused him to react so sharply. Whatever it was, instinct told her it was bad. Her hand had reached for the door handle several times, only to pull back. She couldn't leave Rory alone. Someone might still be watching, and he was defenseless.

And Dan had told her to stay. Normally, her stubborn streak might have resisted being told what to do. But he had used the tough voice she thought of as his cop voice. The one that said the situation was serious. She had learned in the past few days to trust that voice and do what it said.

Out of the corner of her eye, she saw movement as Jace and Dan rounded the corner. They stopped short of the car. It seemed like forever before Dan nodded and headed toward her. Jace headed back to where Dan had first stopped. He took a few pictures of something on the ground, then tapped something on his phone.

That was it. Dan had told her to stay, but he was back now. And she needed to know why they weren't getting a move on. Her mother was missing. And her daughter was at the police station.

She had had enough.

After pushing the door open and getting out, she stalked over to Dan. Hands on her hips, she waited for him to acknowledge her. He met her eyes reluctantly.

"Dan? What's going on?"

"Mags." He stopped.

She squeaked when he suddenly grabbed her in a fierce hug. It was hard to breathe, he held her so tight. And he was scaring her.

She used her hands to push back, creating space between them.

"Dan, tell me what's wrong!"

"We found a trail, Maggie. I'm pretty sure it's blood."

Blood? But that meant...

"Mom? He hurt my mom?"

Dan grabbed her by both arms. Not hard. Just enough to steady her. She was on the edge of dissolving into hysterics. Focusing on Dan helped her to step back off the ledge.

"I don't know what it means. Yes, she could be hurt. Or maybe her attacker was hurt. Or maybe it happened earlier and no one noticed it. Whatever the case may be, I need you to let me do my job so we can find her. Clear?"

Words were beyond her at that point, so she satisfied herself with nodding.

"Good. Look, we are going to be a little while." He reached back and took out his phone. "Take my phone, call Paul. Number two, remember? I'm sure he'll let you talk with Melanie, just to get an idea of what's happening at the station."

She clutched his phone to her chest. Right now it felt like a lifeline.

"Are you sure you won't need it?"

"I'll use Jace's if I need to call someone. Go ahead. Sit in the car." He turned and strode back around the side of the house.

Shoving her hands into the pocket of her hoodie, she scurried back to the car. In her haste to talk with Melanie, she wasn't aware at first of the car purring up the driveway. Her head jerked up when two men jumped out of it and raced toward her. Fear paralyzed her for an instant, then she gathered her wits enough to open her mouth and scream. It was cut off almost instantly by a rough slap. Tears stung her eyes. For a second her vision was blurry. Hard arms grabbed her from behind and started dragging her.

"You want to see your mama alive again you need to come with us." She shivered at the angry voice snarling in her ear. Her mother was alive? Maybe he was lying, though. These people were obviously willing to kill. Lying wouldn't be that hard.

Instinct had her struggling to free herself. She kicked back and heard a grunt as her heel connected with a leg. It awarded her a small spurt of satisfaction. Short-lived satisfaction.

"Enough or we hurt the kid."

Rory!

"I'll go. Leave him alone."

Without another word she was dragged to their car. She wasn't even given the choice of walking. Fear like she had never known grew inside her. She was going to die. Her children would grow up without her. Who would raise them? Would her mother be set free?

Dan would never know that she loved him. Now that she was going to die, she regretted never being brave enough to tell him.

The front door slammed open. An officer she recognized as Tony ran out and charged at them, his revolver ready. The man holding her tightened his grip. The other raised his gun and fired. Horrified, she watched as Tony stumbled and fell. Then he was still.

A shout rang out. Dan raced around the side of the house, Jace only a step behind him.

The gunman shot. Missed. Dan and Jace separated. The shooter had two targets now, coming from two different angles, and he couldn't seem to decide which one to aim at first—buying them a few seconds.

"Dan!" The scream burst from her. He had to be careful. He had to. The man holding her switched his hold, placing an arm around her neck. She gurgled as his hold tightened. She bit his hand. He swore, slapped her. Her head whipped to the side.

Dan was almost upon them. He raised his gun again. Another bullet rang out from the gunman's weapon. Dan flew back. In slow motion, she saw him. Falling. Falling.

Jace yelled, but her ears seemed to be stuffed with cotton. Pain and grief exploded inside her.

"Dan!" she shrieked.

She saw the meaty fist coming but didn't have time to duck.

Agony. Then darkness.

SIXTEEN

A motor was running. She could feel it rumbling beneath her head. She opened her eyes. Everything was dark. She wiggled. Her hands were tied behind her back. She was lying on her side on some kind of rough blanket. Sniffing, she scrunched up her nose in disgust. It was damp and moldy.

Moving her head, she winced as her jaw ached. She worked it back and forth. It probably wasn't broken, even though pain shivered through her face when she opened her mouth more than an inch. She vaguely remembered being punched. Right after...

Dan! Fresh agony ripped through her. In her mind she saw him falling again and again. Bile clawed its way up her throat. She gasped, struggling to keep it down. Was he alive? *Oh, Lord, please let him be alive. Please let me live long enough to tell him that I love him.* And her babies! What had happened to Rory? And who had Siobhan now?

She was helpless to hold back a sob. Tears fell down her face, dripping off onto whatever surface she was lying on.

Someone moaned just inches away. Her breath froze.

"Mom?" she whispered. She could barely hear, her heart was pounding so hard.

"Maggie? Is that you?"

Gratitude welled up inside her. Her mom was alive, and they were together. For now. They were definitely in a dangerous situation.

"I'm here, Mom. Not sure where here is, though."

Movement. It sounded as though her mom was wrestling against her bindings.

"It's no use. I can't get loose," her mother exclaimed. "I think we are on some kind of vehicle. I feel like we're moving."

"Trunk of a car?" The space did have an enclosed feeling. The air felt thin around her.

"No," her mother answered. "The area is small, but not that small."

A sudden jolt halted their conversation. Two doors slammed. Her insides quivered. Footsteps. One set on either side. Behind her, she heard her mother's breathing become harsher. Faster.

The footsteps stopped. She could hear the murmur of voices but was unable to decipher any individual words. It was almost like listening from inside a bubble.

The covering was whipped back. Agony seared through her head as the sunlight flared bright in her unprotected eyes. She blinked rapidly, trying to focus. The men in front of her were nothing but blobs as her eyes struggled to adjust. Her head continued to pound. An evil chuckle polluted the air.

"Looks like our guests are ready to join us. Come on, ladies. The boss wants to meet you."

Rough hands grabbed her and yanked her from the vehicle. She wobbled as she was set down on her feet.

Painful tingles shot up her numb legs. She started to crumble. Hard hands caught her and the man holding her chuckled again. He shifted his hold and something in her pocket pressed against her stomach. Dan's cell phone!

"Guess you won't be kicking anyone now."

That was right. She had kicked the foul man before. How she wished for the strength to struggle enough to kick him again! She was too weak even to stand upright, though. Her eyes focused enough to look around as the other man pulled her mother out. They had been in the back of a pickup truck covered with a tarp. They were on a dock. A large boat bobbed gently on the waves. Lake Erie. She had always thought the lake was spectacular. Right now, the only feeling the lake inspired was alarm.

They were herded onto the boat, half dragged and half carried down the stairs. A man was standing with his back to them, staring out the small window. He made no move to acknowledge them as they were shoved into the room and deserted by their captors.

Maggie glanced at her mother, wincing at the sight of the cut across her mother's forehead. That explained the blood Dan had found. Anna offered her a smile and glanced up, closing her eyes briefly. Then she cocked an eyebrow at her daughter. Maggie thought her mother was telling her to pray. Nodding to show she understood, she attempted to do just that. Only, no words came to mind. Finally, she settled for praying *Help, Lord.* Over and over she repeated the simple litany in her mind.

The man at the window apparently decided they had waited long enough. He turned and graced them with a mocking little bow. He was a handsome man in his midforties, of medium height and slightly stocky. His brown hair was short. His eyes—had she ever seen such cold eyes?—like ice. He smiled at her. A beautiful smile that sent shivers down her spine. He reminded her of a tiger ready to pounce. His face was one she had seen in pictures, but never in person. Yet she knew she would never forget it, even if she somehow escaped this situation alive.

This was Gary Chambers.

His eyes settled on Anna. His smile disappeared. "You, madam, were a mistake. I had no desire to kidnap you. However, the mistake was made, and you will have to suffer the consequences along with your daughter."

Anna paled but kept her face serene. If Maggie had ever forgotten how strong her mother was, she was reminded now. Even facing death, Anna kept her cool. Maggie would do her best to emulate her.

His gaze returned to Maggie, and she forced herself to meet it squarely. His lip curled in a sneer. "You. I had originally thought that once I had the information your despicable husband had stolen, I would let you live. Probably let you see firsthand the business your husband was undermining."

She shuddered at the thought of being forced into the human trafficking ring he controlled.

"It's too late now. For you. Do you know how much time and money I have wasted searching for you?" He glared, a muscle twitching in his cheek. "Purchard was easy to convince. He had a sick mother in assisted living. I helped him out when he couldn't afford a bill, and he returned the favor. But the others were far more costly. And for what? The cops have raided my offices.

Frozen my assets and my bank accounts. My business associates are turning on me, cutting themselves deals in return for information on me." He bent his head to the side and spat. The venom in his voice made her hair stand on end.

"I have other accounts, of course. Other sources of income that the feds don't know about. So I can disappear. But you, Maggie Slade, will pay for the misery you have caused me."

So that's why she was still alive. He wanted his revenge.

"I never knew what Malcolm was involved with," she began. He stepped closer and pushed his face next to hers. So close her eyes began to cross. She reared back.

"I don't care. You were his wife. And between the two of you, you've destroyed me. I spent years building up this business, achieving the life I wanted, and now it's gone. Gone!" The last word was bellowed in her face, his rancid breath nearly choking her.

He pushed a button. A minute later, his goons reappeared. He headed up the stairs and the men each grasped one of the women and pulled her along. But this time they struggled, kicking and twisting with all their might.

It was useless. Within moments, they were on the deck. Was he planning on shooting them? Drowning them? Frantically, she looked around, hoping to see another boat, or someone walking along the dock. No one. It was fall. Very few people came out on cold days such as this. Her hope dwindled.

"Go out deeper," Chambers directed one of his men. The man dipped his head and headed to the front. Soon they were speeding toward the middle of the lake.

"I considered just shooting you, but I'm not fond of blood. I almost had my associates construct a way to make your deaths look like an accident. But what was the point? The police already know that I'm the person after you." His manner was almost friendly now, which made the current situation even more terrifying. "I decided drowning would be more suitable. I wanted you to be aware of what was happening. And I wanted you to understand why. Then my revenge will be complete."

He slipped an arm around Maggie's shoulders. She quivered in fear and disgust. Casually, he started pushing her toward the edge of the boat. Anna cried out in distress and moved to intercept them. The man behind her yanked her back.

Maggie tripped and started to fall. Chambers held on to her. A dip in the boat unbalanced them both and sent them to the ground. Growling, he stood and started dragging her toward the rail of the boat.

Maggie fought with all her strength, but it was fading fast. It was over.

Dan drove toward Lake Erie as fast as he could. He had awoken as the paramedics were loading him onto a stretcher. Another ambulance had already taken Tony to the hospital. There had been no word yet on his condition. But there was no way Dan was going to the hospital. It was ironic that Seth and he had that in common on the same day.

Seth. He had wanted to follow Maggie, to try to help Dan rescue her. Dan had refused, knowing an untrained man with a concussion would only be in the way. Instead, he asked her frantic brother to take his nephew back to the station and look after him and Siobhan until

Dan could bring Maggie back. Alive. He refused to even consider that she would die. What would he do if she died?

"Lieutenant Willis?"

He punched the button on his radio. "Yeah, Chief."

"We have the coordinates from your phone's GPS. Looks like they are on a boat heading out into Lake Erie. You have my permission to commandeer a boat to go out after them. Jackson and Olsen are on their way to lend assistance."

"Okay, Chief. I'm on my way now." This time he didn't even hesitate to use his siren. Cars pulled to the side of the road as he sped past.

"And, Dan? You use whatever force you need to in order to bring those women home."

Paul knew. Despite how hard Dan had tried to disguise his weakness, Paul knew how hard it was for Dan to pick up his gun. He probably should have felt mortified. But he didn't. He had no room for any emotion that interfered with saving Maggie.

At the dock he persuaded a man who was cleaning out his boat to take him out on the lake. Actually, Dan had whipped out his badge and threatened the man with charges of obstruction of justice to make the man stop arguing. He had grudgingly complied. Granted he wasn't happy about it, but that wasn't Dan's priority. His goal was to get the woman he loved and her mother home. Safe. Two small children were depending on him to bring their mom home. He wouldn't fail them. Not this time. He might fail in the future. It was inevitable. But not this time.

After what seemed like hours he spotted the boat. Something was happening on the deck.

"Hand me those binoculars!" he hollered at the boater.

Muttering, the man passed them over. Dan lifted them to his eyes. And his world screeched to a halt. Gary Chambers was dragging Maggie toward the front of the boat. He could see her struggling. Her legs were flailing, but her arms were bound behind her back. Chambers's intention was clear. He was going to toss her overboard. Let her drown.

"Can't this thing go faster?"

"I'm going as fast as I can." The boater was pale. He, too, was staring at the boat ahead of them.

Sick with horror, Dan saw Chambers heft Maggie's kicking body and throw her into the lake. Her scream was cut off as her head went beneath the water. Chambers had already returned with Anna when Maggie's head popped up above the water. She was choking and gasping. He could tell by the way she bobbed that she was kicking her legs to keep herself afloat. How long could she continue?

Chambers looked up. His eyes widened when he glimpsed the boat speeding toward him. He stopped dragging Anna. He actually pushed her away from him while he grabbed the gun from the man standing next to him and pointed it. Straight at Maggie.

"No!" the criminal screamed. "You need to die! No rescue for you!" His first shot went wild. Maggie ducked under the water. When she popped up again, she had moved several feet closer to Dan's boat.

Chambers screamed out his fury and took aim again.

Dan was going to have to shoot him. For the first time in years, Dan grabbed his gun without dread coursing through him. He didn't have to kill Chambers. Maybe he could wound him. If the man could be brought to justice, Dan would prefer to do it that way.

Chambers jerked the gun to where Maggie was now. Dan could see her energy was already flagging. She had to be exhausted. Plus, Lake Erie was cold this time of year.

Dan squeezed the trigger, aiming for Chambers's left arm. The one holding the gun. Chambers twisted to get a better shot at Maggie, and the bullet took him in the shoulder. He yelled but didn't drop the gun. No, he raised it and again took aim.

Once more, Dan fired. And Chambers fell.

In a flash, Dan dropped his own gun to the deck and dived into the chilly waters. Swimming with every ounce of strength he possessed, he made for Maggie. He could see her starting to sink. With an adrenaline-fed burst of speed, he managed to reach her before she went under.

"Hold on, Mags. I've got you, baby. Stay with me. Come on." Keeping up a steady stream of encouragement, he pulled her back to the boat. His unwilling chauffeur was ready, reaching out to help him pull the drenched and shivering woman on board.

He found some blankets and piled them around her shoulders. Dan instructed the boater to head back to shore. He saw the other police cruiser arrive at the dock and radioed Olsen and Jackson to go and get Anna off the boat. The officers located another motorboat and within minutes had boarded the craft.

His cell phone was gone, probably lying on the bottom of Lake Erie. His now-willing driver handed him his cell phone so Dan could call Jackson for a report.

"Got Mrs. Slade, Lieutenant. And we've apprehended

Chambers's accomplices. They're cuffed and already crying for a lawyer. We're taking them in."

"Chambers?" He held his breath.

"He's dead, sir."

Dan bowed his head. He'd had no choice. He knew that, but taking a life was never something to take lightly.

"Thanks for coming for me."

He lifted his head and saw the most beautiful sight he had ever seen. The woman he loved was alive. He had saved her and made sure that the twins would not be orphans. That was something he could be proud of. Giving in to temptation, he leaned in and kissed her forehead. He stayed for a second to breathe her in.

He still wasn't worthy of her. He knew that now. But at least he knew she would survive.

An ambulance was waiting to carry the women to the hospital. He held Maggie's hand until they loaded the stretcher, then stood watching the road until the vehicle had disappeared.

"Hey, buddy."

Jace had arrived. But something wasn't right. His usually cheerful friend was wearing a grief-stricken expression. Dan's instincts went into high gear. Someone had died. Who...? Oh, no. His gut clenched.

"Tony?"

Jace nodded. A tear wobbled its way down his cheek. He scrubbed the palms of his hands against his eyes. When he took them down, the tears were under control, but the sorrow remained in his expression.

Dan wasn't one to judge. He was fighting his own losing battle against his grief, and he and Tony were just friends. He knew that Jace had been very close with his brother-in-law.

"When?" That was all he could manage. His throat was raw.

"In surgery. He never regained consciousness. Irene…" Jace let the sentence fade away.

Poor girl. Irene would be devastated.

And he had considered telling Maggie he loved her? Now he was glad he hadn't. He was surer than ever that she'd be better off without him.

Maggie wiped a tear from her eye. Tony Martello's funeral was one of the saddest she had ever attended. He had been loved and deeply respected in the small community. The procession from the church to the cemetery had stretched for a mile.

Irene was pale but seemed to be holding herself together. Her small sons held her hands, confusion written all over their freckled faces. At ages two and four, they were too young to understand what was happening.

To her right, she could hear Tony's mother sobbing uncontrollably. The sound ripped through her.

She looked at her twins, nestled safely in her and her mother's arms. They were unusually quiet today, as if they, too, were aware of the sadness of the occasion.

Her eyes shot to the pallbearers. Dan, Paul, Jace, Jackson, Thompson and Olsen stood with their dress uniforms on. Their expressions were stern, but she couldn't help but notice the grief shadowing their faces. It broke her heart to see the agony in Dan's beloved eyes. He looked a little lost. What would this do to him?

The past few days were already taking their toll. Despite the closeness they had initially shared following her rescue, an invisible barrier had gone up between them that was even harder to get past than when they had first met. Oh, sure, Dan was polite. But no more than that. When they met, he was distant. His smiles were infrequent and never quite reached his eyes. And they were all for her children, who continued to adore him.

But he still watched her. She would look up and catch his unguarded gaze. Those gray eyes brimmed with a mixture of longing and despair. She knew he loved her as she loved him. She refused to believe she was wrong about that. But the events of the past few days had created such a wall between them that she wasn't sure love was enough.

What could she do? She couldn't force him to face his demons. All she could do was turn it over to God. It still amazed her that she was praying again. She had lived so long without acknowledging God, sometimes she still felt guilty about asking Him for help. But, she reminded herself, He had never abandoned her. Just like she would never abandon her children. If one of them went astray, she would always accept them back.

Her eyes flashed to her mother. Anna was living proof of this truth. Maggie had apologized several times. And had been met with love and tenderness. No reproofs or reprimands.

God was like that.

The funeral ended and the mourners drifted from the grave site. She had decided to approach Dan after the funeral. Not in a confrontational manner. More like "Hey, how are you? Want to grab a cup of coffee?" That sort of thing.

Her eyes skimmed over the people still hanging

around. Ah. There he was. He seemed to be in a pretty deep conversation with Paul. She mentally rolled her eyes at herself, calling the chief of police by his first name. But he had asked her to. Anyway, their conversation looked serious. She'd have to bide her time and wait until they were done.

Her mother and Seth were walking together, showing off the twins and getting acquainted. That was a strange idea still. But Seth wanted to be a part of her life, so he insisted he needed to be friends with those she loved. And it wasn't as though her mother had meant to come between his parents. If anything, Anna had been another victim of his father's selfishness.

Her eyes moved back to where Dan and Paul had been to see if they'd finished their conversation. Wait a minute! Where had Dan gone? Paul was still there, looking even sadder than before. He saw her staring and sighed. Then he started moving in her direction. Oh, no. Her stomach dropped. She desperately needed a glass of water, because her mouth was suddenly as dry as a desert. Whatever Paul was coming over to say, it wasn't good.

Instinctively, she shook her head in denial. He stopped in front of her. It seemed to take a huge effort on his part to speak, so she went first.

"He's gone, isn't he?" Her voice was harsh.

He nodded, his expression somber.

She pressed her lips together so they wouldn't tremble. Blinking rapidly, she focused her attention over his shoulder. Maybe she could find him before he got too far. A hand on her shoulder brought her back.

"Let him go, Maggie," Paul implored. "He needs time. A little space to get his act together."

"Will he come back?" she demanded. Part of her was amazed at her own boldness.

"I don't know." Not what she wanted to hear. "I hope he will. He knows he's welcome. There's nothing more than that I can do."

She hesitated to ask the next question. Because really, what was the point if he was going to leave without even saying goodbye?

"Do you know where he's going?"

"No. He didn't say, and I didn't ask."

So that was it. It was over before it had even started. But she knew she'd never forget him. He'd left and taken her heart with him.

SEVENTEEN

Maggie took one last look at herself in the mirror and decided she was ready to go. She grabbed her winter coat and her gloves and headed downstairs. Giggles and shrieks echoed through the house. She grinned as she entered the living room, where Seth was being tackled by two very wound-up toddlers. A grin she quickly repressed.

"You know I'll never get them to bed on time tonight, right?" She aimed a mock glare at her unrepentant brother.

Seth beamed back at her. "Take it easy, sis. Uncle Seth will have these two munchkins clean and ready for bed when you get home."

She couldn't help it. She smiled at him, her heart welling up with tenderness. She loved it when he called her sis. He had taken his role as brother and uncle to heart. Even to the point of acting as her babysitter when she needed to go out. He spoiled the kids, but Maggie didn't have the heart to discourage him. She understood that part of his actions was making up for the times she had struggled without her brother to look after her. It was crazy, but it was always heartbreakingly sweet the way he'd taken brotherhood in stride. His father, or rather their father, was still trying to come to terms with the whole here's-your-grown-daughter scenario. Although she no longer hated her father, she was still glad that he never invited her to call him Dad. They both seemed to be satisfied with Joe.

"Okay, I'm going." Giving her kids a quick kiss and Seth a hug, she walked out to her car, noticing that Seth had cleared the snow off and started it for her. He'd shoveled the driveway, too. Her eyes grew damp. She just wasn't used to anyone taking care of her.

After getting in the car, she backed carefully down the driveway of the comfortable two-story house she lived in with the twins. The roads weren't bad after the previous night's snow, just a little wet. She steered cautiously onto the main road and headed into town. In a few hours it would be dark. The Christmas lights would come on. She should start thinking about getting a tree. Probably a fake one, since a real tree was a lot of work. Seth would be willing to help out, but it wasn't *his* help she craved.

Sighing, she pulled into the restaurant parking lot and turned off the motor. And continued to sit, her head bent. Two months. It had been two months since Dan had walked away. Two months without a word. Of course, her mother was always willing to listen to her when the sorrow overwhelmed her. Her friends had tried to be there for her, to support her. It was weird, but Mel and she had become close. It had been a long time since she had allowed herself the luxury of a best friend. In fact, with the exception of Wendy, it had been a long time since she'd had a friend at all. But even Mel couldn't answer the questions she needed the answers to. How was he? Was he recovering? Would he ever come back?

Every morning, she prayed for Dan. Sometimes she caught herself looking out the window and dreaming about him.

Her twins helped her through the worst days. But when she was alone, the ache grew. She had loved her husband, but now she realized it was a selfish kind of love. It was a love born out of the need for human companionship. After finding out the truth about her father and blowing up at her mother, she'd needed to feel loved and valued by someone. If she had had the support of the friends that she had now, she may not have fallen for him. But Dan…Dan was the other half of her heart. She remembered how natural it had felt just to sit silently with him. How he would take her hand and squeeze it when she was upset or sad. She remembered how he had willingly put himself in harm's way to protect her and the children. Every time.

Enough! Throwing open the door of her sedan, she picked her way across the parking lot, taking care to avoid any black ice. She entered the restaurant and was greeted with the aromas of a variety of delicious foods. The warmth enfolded her like a hug. She'd often come to this restaurant before her troubles started. The young hostess smiled a greeting and seated her.

"A woman is meeting me here," she informed the hostess, accepting the menu she was handed. "My name is Maggie."

"Fine. I will bring your guest over when she arrives." The hostess smiled again and left.

Five minutes later, she returned with a tall, slim woman. Lily Klemz was just as Dan had described her. Glamorously beautiful, despite the long scar running down the left side of her face. Her blond hair was styled with casual elegance and her makeup was flawless. She settled herself across from Maggie. Both had yet to say a word. A bubbly waitress, most likely a college student, set glasses of water in front of them and departed again, promising to return soon for their orders.

The awkward silence settled between them. How exactly did one start a conversation with the ex-wife of one's dead husband? Maggie risked a glance at Lily's elegant face. Any awkwardness she felt was overshadowed by the sympathy she experienced when pain flashed briefly across the other woman's face. She wasn't as calm as she looked.

"Thank you for meeting me here, Lily." Lily startled at Maggie's softly spoken words, although she must have expected Maggie to say something.

"I don't know why you wanted to meet," Lily blurted before her red-painted lips pressed together. Probably to disguise the fact that they were trembling.

"I wanted you to have something." Maggie reached into her purse and pulled out an envelope, which she slid across the table. Lily slowly opened it and peered inside. She blanched and started shaking. In her hand she held a check. A very large check.

The young waitress came by. Mostly to give the other woman time to recover, Maggie ordered first. Just a Diet Coke and salad. Nerves were rumbling through her stomach like a power drill. There was no way she could eat much of anything.

"And for you, ma'am?"

Lily shook her head.

The young girl waited. Really? She couldn't see that Lily was distressed?

"That'll be all for now." Maggie smiled at the girl, silently willing her to leave quickly.

When she was gone, Lily lifted her head. Maggie's heart went out to her. Lily's blue eyes were swimming in tears.

"What is this?" Lily managed to choke out.

"Malcolm, the man I knew as Phillip, was a wealthy man by the time he died. I asked, and the money is clean." Maggie reached across the table to touch Lily's hand with her own. "Lily, I know you suffered because of our husband's business, and so did I. So when the money was handed over to me, how could I keep it all?"

In fact, she had kept less than half. It made sense to her, since she had already taken some when she had gone into hiding.

"So, was it all for nothing?"

Maggie heard the note of anger in Lily's voice and frowned, puzzled.

"Was what for nothing?"

Lily waved an elegant hand at the envelope. "The second job, the trouble Malcolm got himself into. If he had so much money, why would he need to get involved in any of that? Why keep it from me?"

"No, Lily," Maggie hastened to explain. "Believe me, I asked the same questions. The money was made after all that. Part of it was that he saved everything he could while working at the job the Witness Protection people got him. He also did do some investing. Apparently, he would invest and pull his money when he had made a large profit. He did that for several years running. I can't explain it any better than that."

After grabbing her water, Lily swallowed a couple sips. Maggie thought more to give herself time to think than because she was truly thirsty. Better let her have a moment, although it was difficult to sit and wait. Finally, Lily met her eyes again.

"You could have kept it all. I never would have known anything about it."

She nodded. What else could she say? Besides, she didn't think the blonde sitting across from her really expected an answer. Lily confirmed it when she continued without waiting for a response.

"I appreciate it. I really do. Life hasn't been easy, and this will help. So I thank you for your kindness." Sliding out of the booth, Lily stood and buttoned her coat, then slid leather gloves onto her hands. Picking up the envelope, she slid it into her large purse.

"Please don't take this the wrong way, Maggie. I mean no disrespect, and I don't hold a grudge against you. Maybe if we had met under different circumstances... Well, who knows? But the point is I think it would be best if this was the end of our association."

Nodding, Maggie watched as Lily turned and wove through the restaurant and out the door. She couldn't blame her. Contacting her had definitely fallen outside Maggie's comfort zone. Still, it had been the right thing to do.

Her phone buzzed. She slipped it out of her pocket and saw she had a text from Seth.

Kids clean n fed. Watching a movie. I win best uncle award.

Maggie grinned and replied.

Sure do. Mind if I do some Christmas shopping?

Knock yourself out. My favorite color is green.

Laughing to herself, she put the phone back in her pocket. As the waitress passed, she asked for the bill. The girl gave her a startled look. No wonder. She hadn't even touched her salad. "And a doggie bag," she amended. Maybe she'd eat when she got home.

While waiting for the check, she turned her thoughts to a more positive subject. Christmas shopping. Funny how last year she hadn't even bothered. The twins had been too young to know any better, and she'd had no one else to buy for. This year she had a whole host of people. The kids, her mom, Seth, Mel and Jace, maybe even her dad, although she couldn't really think of him as her father. And she'd have to find something that would travel well to send to Wendy, still away on her mission trip—with a new house sitter in place.

A motorcycle outside the window caught her attention. Her breath hitched as memories of Dan again flooded through her. If only he had stayed, they could have celebrated the season together. Her first year as a believer since she was a child. Yes, if only...

"Maggie."

Her heart stuttered, then started racing. Her hands grew cold. Even as she slowly rotated in her seat she scolded herself for being weak, for still wanting to believe that he would come back to her. He was gone. He wasn't coming back...but there he was.

Dan.

* * *

He drank in the sight of her. Black curls, wide blue eyes. Her face seemed a little pale, but it was still the most gorgeous face he had ever seen. How could he have ever been so stupid as to leave her behind? He had thought he was doing the right thing, but looking at her face, he could see his actions had built a wall between them. It wouldn't be easy to break down her defenses.

Good thing he wasn't afraid of a fight. And she was worth it.

Without waiting for permission, he sat down across from her. Her lips pursed and she raised her chin. Nope. She wasn't going to make this easy.

"I'm not staying. I was just on my way out."

Ouch. She could freeze a man with that voice. He winced.

"Please, Mags. I know I messed up. I'm hoping to do better. Hear me out? Please?"

Wariness battled with yearning on her face. His throat tightened. He had missed her so much. What if she didn't feel the same way? What if she wouldn't hear him out?

He wouldn't give up, he reminded himself. If it took him the next five years, he would pester her until she let him in.

"You left," she fairly spat. "After all we had gone through, you just took off without a word. I had to hear you were gone from your chief."

He ducked his head. It was true, and she had the right to be angry.

"I had to, Maggie. I needed to get my head on straight. If I had waited any longer, I would have found an excuse to stay with you and the kids. Please, can we just go somewhere private and talk?"

Maggie didn't answer but grabbed up her coat and shoved her arms into it. She took the bill from the waitress and handed her some money. Dan caught a glance at the check. That big of a tip would have the girl smiling all night. He followed Maggie as she headed out.

"Where are you parked?" Rather than reply, she shot out her arm and hit a button on her key fob. The lights on the four-door sedan directly ahead of them flashed.

"Okay, I'm there." He yanked a thumb over his shoulder at the motorcycle. Her eyes widened. "Yeah, that's the same one we rode on together."

"Well, I'm not getting on that thing again. Not in this weather."

"Fine. Follow me home. We can talk in private there."

Reluctantly, she nodded.

As he led the way back to his apartment, he worried about what to say. "Lord, please give me the words to say."

Ten minutes later, he opened the door for her, hoping he hadn't left a mess. He hadn't planned on bringing her here. He had intended to go to her house and grovel, but things hadn't quite worked out. So he was improvising.

"I should call my house first," she blurted. "Let Seth know where I am."

"He already knows."

Her eyebrows rose.

"I stopped by your house to see you. He told me where you were. Said he would text you and let you know you could take your time." He saw comprehension cross her face. "I could see you were with Lily Klemz, so I waited until she left before I approached you."

She sighed. "Just tell me what you need to tell me so I can go."

Dan ran a hand through his hair. "I was seriously messed up, Maggie. After I shot Chambers, I mean. I hadn't shot anyone since Afghanistan. Suddenly, within days, I had killed two people." He raised his hands to ward off protest. "I had no choice, I know that. I take no pleasure in what I had to do, but I know that I had to do it. Faced with those circumstances, I'd do it again. But still, it put me right back in Afghanistan. And then Tony died, and I felt that was my fault, too. That I had screwed up."

Cool hands framed his face. Shocked, Dan jerked back. Maggie followed.

"That had nothing to do with you. Remember, you were shot, too."

He held both her hands to his face briefly, shutting his eyes. He had been afraid she would never touch him again. He nodded.

"I know that now. I have been in therapy for two months. Post-traumatic stress disorder. That's what my therapist diagnosed me with." His eyes opened when he heard her suck in a breath. "I knew I needed help. I explained the situation to Paul and he agreed. I took a medical leave of absence, because I sure wasn't gonna do anyone any favors as a cop until I worked through my issues. And then there was you. I could never even think of staying in your life until I straightened myself out. Not just for you, but for your kids, too."

Carefully, afraid she would pull away, he leaned down and let his forehead rest against hers. Her perfume, flowers and spice, rose up to meet him. He inhaled deeply. "You deserve a man who is whole. And they deserve a father who can be there for them completely, without reservations. Maggie, I want to be that man. But I couldn't before. I wasn't ready. I'm still in therapy, and I might be for a while. But I love you. And I love your kids. I know you have no reason to believe me. And maybe you won't feel the same way about me. But I would like the chance to try."

Somehow her hands had left his face and had crept around to the back of his neck. Her touch warmed him all the way through, melting the ice of fear that had remained around his heart. Warm, cinnamon-scented breath fanned his face. He was scared to move in case it was all a dream.

"I missed you so much, Dan. Every day was filled with thoughts of you. Whenever the twins did something new, I would think, if only Dan could see this." Tears glistened on her long lashes, but a smile trembled on her lips. "When you showed up tonight, I was tempted to resist. I didn't want my heart broken again. I couldn't, though. I remember being on that horrible boat with Chambers, thinking I was going to die, wishing you knew that I loved you. I was terrified, but I knew I would always regret not giving you a chance."

He stilled. "So *are* you going to give us a chance?"

Soft laughter slipped past her lips. She tugged on his neck. He was only too happy to comply. He brushed her lips softly with his. They both sighed. Their lips met again, this time for a longer kiss. A kiss filled with forgiveness and healing. He wrapped his strong arms around her and pulled her close.

He had come home.

EPILOGUE

"And now it's time for the bride and groom's first dance together. Please welcome Mr. and Mrs. Willis to the dance floor."

The opening notes of the song they had chosen poured from the speakers.

"They're playing our song, Mrs. Willis," Dan's husky voice murmured in her ear. He swept her onto the dance floor. Maggie was only too happy to follow his lead. It seemed as though she had waited forever for this day. Dimly aware of the crowd gathering around them, she kept her focus on her man. She could see the joy in her heart echoed in his eyes.

The past six months hadn't been easy. Dan had had to undergo intensive therapy. He still visited a therapist, but the frequency had been decreased to once a month. Maggie knew he still suffered from the occasional nightmare. But the flashbacks had ended. He had come to grips with what had happened in Afghanistan, although he would never forget. And he'd come to terms with the lives he'd taken while protecting her.

Her new husband leaned closer.

"I love you, Mags."

Tears prickled at the backs of her eyes. How had she gotten so blessed? Even after years of anger at God, He had blessed her beyond her wildest dreams.

"Love you back."

Soon after, they left the dance floor to stroll among their guests. Maggie was astonished at the sheer number of friends she had accumulated in such a short time. Chief Garraway was there with her husband. Maggie had witnessed for herself the affection between Dan and the older woman who had helped him so much. Now she grinned as the older couple left the dance floor, flushed and laughing.

She smiled as she saw Melanie take Jace's hand and place it on her belly. Both their faces grew intense, then they grinned simultaneously. The baby must have moved.

Irene reached over and placed her hand on her sister-in-law's stomach, her own expression misty. Being a widow with young children was hard. Maggie could empathize. Hard to believe Tony had died almost nine months ago. Poor Irene. She was still grieving for Tony, but when Maggie had considered not asking her to be a bridesmaid out of respect for her feelings, Irene had pitched a fit, demanding the right to be part of the joyous occasion.

"Hey, no sad thoughts. Not today."

Maggie shook herself out of her melancholy reverie and smiled at her husband. "Sorry. You're right. I was just thinking of Irene and Tony."

"I figured."

Maggie opened her mouth to respond, but her words choked on a giggle as she looked across the room. Dan followed her gaze and snickered. Senator Travis and Anna were standing side by side, studiously trying to keep polite expressions on their faces while Siobhan stood between them and held on to both their hands. It didn't take much imagination to understand what had happened. Siobhan was excited to have two grandparents. She had two hands, one for each. Neither grandparent wanted to step back, so they were enduring each other's company. Barely.

Maggie tucked her mouth close to Dan's ear. "If this were a romance novel, they would fall in love all over again and live happily ever after."

Dan gave her an oh-please look. "I wouldn't hold out for that."

"No, I know. They would be a disaster together. I'm just glad they are tolerating each other for the sake of the kids."

"And for you, sweetheart."

Maggie considered. "My mom? Yeah. Him? I don't really think he'd go out of his way for me. We'll never have a father-daughter relationship. Sometimes I think he puts up with me because it looks good to voters that he is trying to amend his ways. I'm not sorry, though. At least I got a brother out of the deal."

Speaking of her brother... Ah! There was Seth. Of course. He was sitting with Rory on his lap. Rory had claimed Seth as his.

A glass started tinkling in the back of the room. Like a wave, more joined in as the guests tapped their spoons against the crystal glasses. "Kiss! Kiss!"

Only too happy to comply, Maggie and Dan kissed softly, their hands entwined.

"Me, too!"

They looked up to see Siobhan running their way, her

black curls dancing. Her beaming mouth had chocolate around the edges.

"Kiss Vonnie, too!"

Rory, never one to let his sister go anywhere without him, scampered off Seth's lap and charged behind. "Me!"

A murmur of chuckles flowed through the crowd as the twins skidded to a halt before Maggie and Dan. Siobhan raised her arms imperiously. "Up, Mommy! Daddy! Give Vonnie a kiss, too!" The guests sighed.

Dan leaned over and scooped up the little girl, chocolate and all.

"Mommy! Daddy! Me, too!" Rory said.

Maggie hefted Rory up into her arms and hugged him close, inhaling his sweet little-boy scent. Her eyes met Dan's. Joy and unshed tears mingled. Daddy. Her darlings had a daddy. Her heart melted every time she heard it, and she knew his did, too. Dan planned on adopting them immediately. But from the moment she had mentioned he would soon be their daddy, the twins had taken to calling him that. Which made life a little embarrassing before the wedding. Now? Now it was one more blessing to be cherished.

They kissed each child. Then, still holding the precious toddlers close, they leaned in and their lips met. A camera flashed. Maggie smiled against Dan's lips. Perfect.

* * * * *

Dear Reader,

Thank you for joining me as I returned to LaMar Pond for Maggie and Dan's story. I was touched by the number of readers who contacted me after reading *Presumed Guilty* and told me they wanted to see a story about some of the secondary characters. I knew even while writing *Presumed Guilty* that I wanted to write Dan's story. The idea of an ex-soldier dealing with PTSD while struggling to perform his duties as a police officer tugged at my heart. I couldn't wait to give him a worthy heroine who would see beyond his woundedness and appreciate his strength and integrity. As for Maggie… Well, who doesn't appreciate a feisty mother raising twins on her own? I had so much fun writing about those kids! I also enjoyed watching her regain the faith she had lost as a child.

I hope you enjoyed Dan and Maggie's story. Even though LaMar Pond, Pennsylvania, is a fictional town, it has become very real to me as I write about the people who live there. I am busy working on the next story now, and I hope to be able to share it with you someday.

I love hearing from readers. I can be found at danarlynn.com, facebook.com/WriterDanaLynn and on Twitter (@DanaRLynn).

Blessings,
Dana R. Lynn

COMING NEXT MONTH FROM
Love Inspired® Suspense

Available March 1, 2016

NO ONE TO TRUST • by Melody Carlson
After Jon Wilson is injured while rescuing Leah Hampton from an attacker on the beach, they run for their lives. Now, as they encounter danger around every corner, they must uncover why someone wants them dead.

PROTECTING HER DAUGHTER
Wrangler's Corner • by Lynette Eason
Someone is trying to kidnap Zoe Collier's daughter, Sophia, and she will risk anything to keep her child safe. And Aaron Starke, the veterinarian she met while in hiding, is determined to do the same.

MISTAKEN TARGET • by Sharon Dunn
Hiding out at an island resort after his cover is blown, FBI informant Diego Cruz is forced to flee with Samantha Jones when an assassin, confusing their cabins, inadvertently attacks Samantha instead of him.

COVERT CARGO
Navy SEAL Defenders • by Elisabeth Rees
When Beth Forrester finds a terrified child wandering next to her lighthouse, she unwittingly becomes the target of a Mexican cartel. And only Dillon Randall, an undercover navy SEAL, can save her.

SUDDEN RECALL • by Lisa Phillips
CIA agent Sienna Cartwright's last mission left her with amnesia. So she turns to her former boyfriend Deputy US Marshal Jackson Parker as she tries to regain her memories...and stay ahead of the people who want to make sure she never remembers her past.

LAST STAND RANCH • by Jenna Night
When Olivia Dillon retreats to a family ranch after making a powerful enemy, trouble follows her. And she must depend on Elijah Morales—a neighboring rancher and former army ranger—for protection.

LISCNM0216

REQUEST YOUR FREE BOOKS!

2 FREE RIVETING INSPIRATIONAL NOVELS
PLUS 2 FREE MYSTERY GIFTS

Love Inspired®
SUSPENSE
RIVETING INSPIRATIONAL ROMANCE

YES! Please send me 2 FREE Love Inspired® Suspense novels and my 2 FREE mystery gifts (gifts are worth about $10). After receiving them, if I don't wish to receive any more books, I can return the shipping statement marked "cancel." If I don't cancel, I will receive 4 brand-new novels every month and be billed just $4.99 per book in the U.S. or $5.49 per book in Canada. That's a savings of at least 17% off the cover price. It's quite a bargain! Shipping and handling is just 50¢ per book in the U.S. and 75¢ per book in Canada.* I understand that accepting the 2 free books and gifts places me under no obligation to buy anything. I can always return a shipment and cancel at any time. Even if I never buy another book, the two free books and gifts are mine to keep forever.

123/323 IDN GH5Z

Name _____ (PLEASE PRINT) _____

Address _____ Apt. # _____

City _____ State/Prov. _____ Zip/Postal Code _____

Signature (if under 18, a parent or guardian must sign) _____

Mail to the **Reader Service:**
IN U.S.A.: P.O. Box 1867, Buffalo, NY 14240-1867
IN CANADA: P.O. Box 609, Fort Erie, Ontario L2A 5X3

**Are you a current subscriber to Love Inspired® Suspense books
and want to receive the larger-print edition?
Call 1-800-873-8635 or visit www.ReaderService.com.**

* Terms and prices subject to change without notice. Prices do not include applicable taxes. Sales tax applicable in N.Y. Canadian residents will be charged applicable taxes. Offer not valid in Quebec. This offer is limited to one order per household. Not valid for current subscribers to Love Inspired Suspense books. All orders subject to credit approval. Credit or debit balances in a customer's account(s) may be offset by any other outstanding balance owed by or to the customer. Please allow 4 to 6 weeks for delivery. Offer available while quantities last.

Your Privacy—The Reader Service is committed to protecting your privacy. Our Privacy Policy is available online at www.ReaderService.com or upon request from the Reader Service.
We make a portion of our mailing list available to reputable third parties that offer products we believe may interest you. If you prefer that we not exchange your name with third parties, or if you wish to clarify or modify your communication preferences, please visit us at www.ReaderService.com/consumerschoice or write to us at Reader Service Preference Service, P.O. Box 9062, Buffalo, NY 14240-9062. Include your complete name and address.

LIS15

SPECIAL EXCERPT FROM

Love Inspired.
SUSPENSE

With a dirty cop out to silence them forever, strangers
Leah Hampton and Jon Wilson must depend on each
other to survive.

Read on for a sneak preview of
NO ONE TO TRUST
by *Melody Carlson*.

Leah Hampton felt her stomach knot as she watched the
uniformed officer in her rearview mirror. His plump
face appeared flushed and slightly irritated in the late
afternoon sun. Glancing around the deserted dune area,
as if worried someone else was around, he adjusted his
dark glasses and sauntered up to her old Subaru. She'd
noticed the unmarked car several miles back but hadn't
been concerned. She hadn't been speeding on this
isolated stretch of beach road—her car's worn shocks
couldn't take it.

Getting out of her car, she adjusted her running tank and
smoothed her running shorts, forcing an optimistic smile.
"Hello," she said in a friendly tone. "I was just heading
out for a beach run. Is something wrong, Officer?"

"Is that your car?"

"Yep." She nodded at her old beater. "And I know I
wasn't speeding."

"No…" He slowly glanced over his shoulder again.
What was he looking for? "You weren't speeding."

"So what's up?" She looked around, too. "Is there

some kind of danger out here? I mean, I do get a little concerned about jogging alone this time of day, especially down here where there's no phone connectivity. But I love this part of the beach, and I'm training for the Portland marathon and it's hard to get my running time in."

"You'll need to come with me," he said abruptly.

"Come with you?" She stared into the lenses of his dark sunglasses, trying to see the eyes behind them, but only the double image of her own puzzled face reflected back at her. "Why?"

"Because I have a warrant for your arrest."

"But you haven't even checked my ID. You don't know who I am." She held up her wallet, but before she could remove her driver's license, he smacked her hand, sending the wallet spilling to the ground.

"Doesn't matter who you are," he growled, "not where you're going."

Don't miss
NO ONE TO TRUST by Melody Carlson,
available March 2016 wherever
Love Inspired® Suspense books and ebooks are sold.

www.LoveInspired.com

"What are you doing here?" she asked as she stretched. When she straightened, he was leaning against the side of his truck, watching her.

"I would have gone running with you if you'd called," he said.

She lifted one shoulder. "I like to run alone."

That was what had changed about her in the years since she'd been sent away. She'd gotten used to being alone.

"Of course." He sat on the tailgate of his truck. "I was driving through town and I saw you running. I didn't like the idea of leaving you here alone."

"I'm a big girl. No one needs to protect me or rescue me."

The words slipped out and she wished she'd kept quiet. Not that he would understand what she meant. He wouldn't guess that she'd waited for him to rescue her from her aunt Mavis, believing he'd show up and take her away.

But he hadn't rescued her. There hadn't been a letter or a phone call. Not once in all of those years had she ever heard from him.

"Sam?" The quiet, husky voice broke into her thoughts.

She faced the man who had broken her fifteen-year-old heart.

"Remington, I don't want to do this. I don't want to talk about what happened. I don't want to figure out the past. I'm building a future for myself. I have a job I love. I have a home, my family and a life I'm reclaiming. Don't make this about what happened before, because I don't want to go back."

He held up his hands in surrender. "I know. I promise, I'm here to talk about the future. Sit down, please."

"I don't want to sit."

"Stubborn as always." He grinned as he said it.

"Not stubborn. I just don't want to sit down."

"I'm sorry they sent you away," he said quietly. In the distance a train whistle echoed in the night. His words were soft, shifting things inside her that she didn't want shifted. Like the walls she'd built up around her.

"Me, too." She rubbed her hands down her arms. "I wasn't prepared to see you today."

She opened her mouth to tell him more but she couldn't. Not yet. Not tonight.

Don't miss
THE RANCHER'S FIRST LOVE by Brenda Minton
available March 2016 wherever
Love Inspired® books and ebooks are sold.

www.LoveInspired.com